Spidey Legs Lana

Black Widow

Book 2

Tessa LaRock

 Send any correspondence or request for information to Amira Rock Publishing, 31 High Street, Felton, Pennsylvania 17322.
Visit "http://www.amirarockpublishing.com"
Cover Art by: Mark Reimann

Printed in the United States of America

Amira Rock Publishing

Spidey Legs Lana ***Black Widow***
is dedicated to
Christine Hocker and Candice Runk.
I am so proud of you both.

Chapter 1

Return

Ches Starling briefly glanced back at Marty Brow and Booger Sheats who stood behind his vehicle. His concern wasn't so much with them, but with the two dark creatures that were in attack position approximately fifty feet away from the front of his jeep.

"Is either of them Evan?" he whispered to Lana as he slowly and carefully released her and sat upright in his seat.

Her voice trembled as she answered, "No."

Ches felt for the large bowie knife tucked beside his seat. And, without turning to face the two males behind them, he shouted, "You can't have her."

"Oh, we're not askin'; we're just doin'," Marty retorted. "You don't have a choice."

"Well, by the looks of it, someone's already kicked your sorry ass. I just hate having to add to your pain by breaking your other arm."

Marty's face twisted in rage as he stepped forward. "Spence, do I have to take this guy's crap? He needs to shut up!"

"Thank you," Ches whispered beneath his breath. "That's exactly what I wanted to know—who I'm fighting against." He then whispered to Lana again.

"Do you know who the other black widow might be?"

After a brief moment Lana answered. "Yes, the other one is Colette—I can tell by her smell."

Ches looked at her strangely.

"Well, we're gonna' need some back up," Ches motioned with his eyes toward his cell phone. It rested in a slot in the dash. "I'm gonna' try and outrun them, but the chances are they'll catch us. You need to call the police—

"No, we can't!" Lana whispered. "They'll find out that I'm a black widow also."

Ches thought about that for a second then replied, "Then, call Trey."

Evan Labonte sat quietly on the couch in his living room. The front door to the cabin was shut tight and the room was dark except for the light coming from the small television set that sat in the corner of the room. The sound was turned down and an old 1950s movie about a gangster outsmarting the law was showing; they were in the midst of a shoot 'em up scene with the police. Evan didn't care much for television; it seemed to be the same old thing—detective shows, sitcoms or reruns.

He got up and switched the television set off. The room became pitch black; however, he was able to see everything clear as day with the ability of his arachnid sight. He stood in silence and slowly looked around. It was still early.

"This is insane," he mumbled to the darkness. "Lana's gone. She's with someone else who can give her more—more of a human life—not the life of a damn insect."

Suddenly, the cabin seemed restricting, unbearably suffocating—he needed to breathe. The urge to transform, change into the arachnid, which was a vast hidden part of his being, was becoming enticing, tantalizing. Angrily, he grabbed his boots and slipped them on. "No! I won't do it. I'm still a human damnit! I want to be a human and do human things!"

Evan shoved through the front door and made his way outside. The sun was shining brightly and the warm breeze felt good against his face. It was Sunday and there was no work today at the construction company, so he needed something to do, something to occupy his time and his mind. The wood was all stacked and piled high for the coming winter and the grass had just been mowed. However, the roof needed some repair. That's what he would do, repair the roof.

Evan retrieved his tool belt from inside, then strapped it around his waist. He then proceeded to remove his t-shirt to enjoy the warmth of the sun's afternoon rays as they beat against his shoulders and back. This part of being human he liked.

Quickly scaling the side of the cabin, he hopped onto the roof. He looked around at the damage that had been done by time and the harshness of winter. *Hmm.*

He thought. *This may take a few hours. Good.* Walking to the other side of the roof, he narrowed his sights in and scanned the horizon.

He could see all of Brenton Forest which sat just two miles away. The forest was lush with vegetation; its leafy trees swaggered nonchalantly in the gentle breeze, flourishing with the fullness of their vibrancy and magnificence. And, amongst their stout and powerful trunks, leading to deep-set roots buried far beneath the earth, were plant life and animals that roamed and romped with ease. It was like a fairy-tale playground for both, where an abundance of energy and liveliness thrived.

Evan frequented the forest often. It was one place he felt comfortable in his arachnid form. There he was respected, revered, yet also, feared as a mighty hunter; not like here in the human world where he was hunted, tracked and considered a hideous beast. It had been that way since he was seven, when he was bitten by a diseased black widow spider that had been poisoned by the military's dumping of chemicals.

Evan was then chased from his home for accidentally killing his mother who had been trapped within his webbing. He mourned terribly at her death; however, the will to survive and overcome his terrible fate had kept him alive and pressing onward.

A little over 100 years had passed since then, making him just over one hundred and eight. He kept track of the years, for he knew his birthday would be coming soon and he seemed to age in appearance one year for every ten years of human life. This made him look seventeen if he were completely human; however, unfortunately, he wasn't.

Several hours passed and Evan had made notable progress with the roof. He had replaced some of the wooden shingles, and a piece of the gutter he had installed several years ago which was now rusted. However, there was still a sizable amount of work to be done.

The sun was burning brighter now. Standing and stretching, he thought of how good a root beer float and piece of shoofly pie would be; they were his favorite. Evan swiped an arm across his sweated forehead.

Luckily, the bakery and soda fountain in Tarren were open on Sundays; this would be a treat. It would certainly be worth the walk. The last time he had shoofly pie was when he had rescued Lana from the mob in town.

Well, that was a mistake, he thought. *She didn't need me; she had Ches and Trey.* Evan shook his head. "No," he spoke aloud, "I'm not gonna' think about it." Grabbing his tools, he shoved them into his tool belt then he jumped down off the roof.

Snatching up his t-shirt, he headed inside. It was dark and depressing in the cabin. He would normally like it that way if he were in his spider form; however, right now he wasn't. Right now, he wanted to feel as human as possible. Washing quickly, he headed back outside.

As soon as Evan stepped out onto the porch, he caught the scent of another arachnid's blood. It was faint, almost too weak to detect. However, he could recognize the smell of another black widow for possibly miles.

He had discovered this ability when he was first bitten and a man in town, nearly a mile and a half away, was infected. The smell of the man's arachnid blood was like peanut butter, thick and sticky; it clogged his nostrils for months. Then, suddenly, one day it just disappeared.

The scent of a female black widow was different. Evan could smell a female for nearly three miles. He had realized it when Lana was taken, when he had found her with Spence. His heart banged within his chest as he concentrated on the scent, wanting it to be hers. However, it was strange, foreign to his nose; and, his shoulders slumped in disappointment at the knowledge that it wasn't.

Then, who was it?

Quickly making his way onto the roof, he attempted to get a better view and a stronger whiff. The breeze had picked up slightly; and, drawing a deep breath, he inhaled through his nose.

The air was warm and summery as it filled his nostrils; it was thick with millions of odors and scents—the smell of fresh cut grass, the moist verdure of the forest, cattle in the distance and an abundance of other things.

Quickly, he sifted through the barrage of odors and focused on the female. Her scent was much stronger now, more prevalent; *and*, he could also smell a male. He recognized it to be Spence.

Suddenly, he smelled Lana's scent and gasped. It wasn't quite as strong as the other two. She was either farther away or was in her human form; however, he wasn't going to wait to find out which.

Immediately, jumping down from the roof, he removed his tool belt and boots. Then tearing through his clothes, he transformed into the beast.

Trey Yanney was in his garage cleaning the dirt from his car. His cell phone vibrated upon his tool box as its ringer rang out the song, *Animal I Have Become.* A bad feeling stirred within his gut as he picked it up and answered it.

"Hello?"

Lana's frightened voice echoed along the phone grid.

"Trey? Trey!" Lana cried into the phone.

"What's wrong?" he demanded.

"You have to help us!" She immediately added, "Ches and me."

"Where are you?" he barked.

He could hear the voice of his best friend, Ches, in the background. "Tell him we're near the old Hobbs' estate, headed toward the river. And, tell him ta' hurry it up!"

Trey hit the off button on his cell and slid it into his pocket. He then raced into the house and immediately headed into the guest room where all their hunting gear was kept.

All the rifles, shotguns and pistols were locked in large wooden closets he and Ches had built. And, the ammunition was in handmade oak drawers that accentuated the closets perfectly. It looked more like the ammunition's barracks for a military base than sporting goods for two young men in college.

Grabbing the 30.06 rifle and an extra box of bullets from one of the drawers, he slung the gun over his shoulder and headed out toward the garage.

Then, grabbing his car keys hanging on the hook just inside the garage door, he jumped in his car, started it and hurriedly backed out.

"Ches, you knucklehead."

"Call disengage," Ches stated loudly in Lana's direction. His call to Trey immediately disconnected.

He and Lana were now traveling at high speed, away from the Hobbs' estate and in the direction of the river. Just moments earlier he had nearly run down Marty Brow, who had thrown his baseball bat at the vehicle and missed, and Booger Sheats who had made a meager endeavor to attack with a ball and chain. Both had scattered like rabbits in an attempt to get out of Ches's way as he floored the gas pedal and barreled in reverse in their direction.

Downshifting, Ches slowed the jeep and turned sharp left onto a dirt road leading back toward town.

Spence and Colette, in the form of black widow spiders, were in high pursuit. They moved rapidly across the terrain, scurrying quickly along with the use of every available tree, sign, and object, while utilizing their webbing and incredible agility and speed.

"I can't outrun them!" Ches shouted above the squealing of the wheels and roaring of the motor. "Can you drive?"

"I guess; but, I don't have my license," Lana anxiously replied, as she recalled having experienced only five hours of driving time in school.

Ches pondered her reply momentarily then responded, "It'll be okay. Just slide over here onto my seat; and, no matter what, just keep your foot on the gas. Drive as far as you can back the way we came, toward town. If you stall, get out and run. I'll hold them off as long as I can."

"No! No, you can't, Ches. Please, don't do this!"

His smile was brief, anxious; and, he couldn't hide the various emotions behind his eyes. "It'll be okay." He touched her face.

She shook her head. "No, please..."

Quickly, he unbuckled her seat belt as she robotically squeezed onto his seat beside him.

"Keep your foot on the gas." He carefully slid his foot off the pedal as Lana slid hers on. "Now, just slow down a little so I can jump out."

"I can't let you do this," she cried.

"You have to." Briefly, he fingered a strand of her hair; then, he grabbed his bowie knife and opened his door. Lana reluctantly released the pressure on the gas slightly and the vehicle slowed.

"I'll be right behind you." Though he smiled, worry was a wrenching shadow upon his face. His lips suddenly touched hers. "Promise me you'll stay safe."

With those words, he leapt from the vehicle, hit the ground and rolled. He quickly got to his feet in time to see the jeep race down the dirt road, and out of sight.

His mind racing, Ches surveyed the area which was thickly lined with trees and vegetation; he needed to get up high. A thick oak would do. He quickly climbed the first tree that looked as if it would serve his purpose, and settled onto a thick limb.

Crouching down, he held the bowie knife firmly in his hand. He was well hidden and he could see the entire area from where he was positioned. He knew Spence and Colette were moving quickly. They would discover he had turned off the main road and reach him in a matter of seconds.

Suddenly, he caught his breath as Spence's huge form spun the corner; Colette was right behind him. She wasn't quite the size of Spence; however, he imagined she was strong. And, the bite from a black widow spider, especially a female, could be fatal.

Ches's heart pounded in his chest and the adrenaline rushed through his veins. It forced him to hold steady until Spence was just beneath him.

"Come on, come on," he whispered beneath his breath. "You only have one chance at this." He quickly made the sign of the cross on his chest. "If you're watching over us, it'd be nice if you'd turn that lunatic into a fish." He rolled his eyes toward Heaven. "Just kidding."

Spence was now beneath him.

Ches wiped a bead of sweat from his face; then, he sprung. His blade hit precisely where he wanted it to—in Spence's skull.

Spence shrieked in rage and shook his head; and, rapidly spinning, he dug his fangs deep within Ches's arm.

"Ugghh!" Ches groaned aloud as Spence latched on and poison raced throughout his system. The pain was horrendous, unbearable, and he swung his blade with all his might in an attempt to break free. Then, he made contact with two of Spence's bulging eyes.

Spence reared back and ripped his fangs from Ches's arm.

Ches scrambled for footing and attempted to stay on his feet. Sweat poured from his body and he continued to fight. And, sending several booted kicks to Spence, he again caught him with his blade.

Suddenly, Spence toppled to the road.

Ches bent and gasped for a breath while seconds passed and his knees grew weak. Grabbing at the crimson spot spreading on his shirt sleeve, he suddenly dropped to the ground. He knew he wouldn't last long; his misjudgment would cost him his life.

Colette had stood watching, watching while her mate fought for their prey—a delectable dish they would surely feast on soon. However, when Spence's large form dropped to the ground, she knew she would have to intervene; her hunger and thirst were driving her crazy. Slowly, she stepped in Ches's direction.

Ches stared through a hazy vision at Colette who was just a few yards away. She opened her mouth and exposed her fangs. And, the two billion teeth lining her black gums chattered loudly, excitedly, as if they could already taste the blood they craved—his blood.

Move, his subconscious shouted. *Get up and move!* He struggled to get to his feet, regardless of the severe pain that was rushing throughout his body—the pain that sent tears blasting at the back of his eyes.

Suddenly, Colette was atop him.

"Uggh!" The breath rushed from him and his limbs became numb. She was powerful, fast; and, the poison that Spence had injected into him was destroying his body. He wouldn't be able to hold her off long.

Drawing every bit of his remaining strength, Ches swung his right fist and punched Colette in one of her eyes. She shrieked in pain and drew back long enough for him to wiggle his way out from beneath her. And, taking the opportunity, he scurried for his knife. His hand shook as he rolled and held the blade firmly before him. He also fought unconsciousness.

Colette moved as a blur in his direction. Then, suddenly, she charged.

But, being a newly born black widow and misjudging her weight, she collided with his blade. It raced along her underbelly and sliced through her thick shell. And, as she attempted to rebound, the blade torn along her legs and severed three. Screeching in pain, she immediately dropped to the ground.

Ches gasped for a breath as he dropped to his knees and clutched his stomach. He was soaked with sweat and began to shake.

"Oh, God!" The pain rushing throughout his body was intense, agonizing, and he fought the darkness that was quickly surrounding him. He knew Spence was near, could feel it in his bones.

Suddenly, Spence appeared before him, his fangs dripping with venom and his mind set on revenge.

Ches, Lana thought, *please stay safe.*

Over the roar of the motor's engine, she was able to hear the car closing in behind her. She knew it was Marty and Booger, for after Ches had nearly run them over, she had seen them jump into Marty's car and tear out after Ches and her. Spence and Colette had been leading the pursuit.

Her heart pounded in her chest as she pressed her foot to the gas pedal and gripped the steering wheel tighter within her hands. It appeared to grow thicker and wilder the faster she went; and the vehicle seemed to increase in size, become more aggressive, more powerful. She knew she was going too fast

Control, get it under control, Lana whispered to herself. *You're gonna' wreck.* She frantically glanced in her rearview mirror. The car behind her was getting closer. Marty and Booger's boisterous conversation was beginning to come through loud and clear.

"Sp...Spence...said...we...c...c...can't...lose... them. N...no...matter...what," she heard Booger stutter.

"Well, that girl's drivin' now. I'll definitely be able to catch her," Marty replied excitedly as he drove with one arm. "And, Spence said we can have our way with her too, *if* we catch her."

Lana could hear Booger snicker. She cringed and gripped the wheel tighter.

The vehicle hugged the road, running parallel, and approximately ten feet in proximity to the cliff's edge. She glanced over the steep incline which plunged nearly forty feet straight down to the rushing water.

The memory of her being drug off the edge of the embankment by Spence, and plunging into the river with him, stabbed at her mind. And, the pain and terror of being captured and tortured by him was like a thousand needles puncturing the surface of her skin. All she knew was that she couldn't get caught again.

This time they would kill her.

But, what about Ches? Her thoughts struggled with the idea of turning around and helping him. “I’m supposed to be a black widow too!” she cried aloud. “I have to have some kind of ability that can help, instead of just running away!”

Lana drove the jeep deeper into what seemed like nothingness, with only trees and vegetation now lining each side of the dirt road. She could no longer see the water though it roared loudly in her ears along with the vehicle behind her.

Suddenly, Marty’s Chevy Camaro tapped the rear of the jeep. Lana screamed as the wheel fought wildly to escape her hands and she attempted to keep the vehicle under control.

The engine of the car behind her roared and she was tapped again. The jeep’s wheel ripped from her hands and the vehicle spun uncontrollably sending her crashing through the thick vegetation and heading toward the river’s edge.

Chapter 2

Evan could sense Lana by the beads of fearful perspiration breaking upon her skin and the blood pumping erratically through her veins. She was on the move and she was in danger.

The beast within him pressed onward, using every available ability to pinpoint Lana's location; she was an arachnid female and his male arachnid senses would spiral in proficiency in search of her.

He could sense that she was just south of the Hobbs' estate, running the old dirt road that ran along the river and back toward town. His senses picked up the pounding of her heart within her chest and her quickened intakes of breath. He was getting closer.

"Damn you, Ches! You and your buddy, Trey, were supposed to keep her safe. What kinda mess you have her in now?" Suddenly, he heard her scream. She was just ahead.

Springing into the air, he shot webbing before him to propel himself through the trees. But suddenly, he was slammed backward as the jeep shot through the trees and crashed into his body.

The force was like two rhinos colliding as Evan hit the tow winch and his webbing snapped. Tumbling backward, he fell over the edge of the cliff.

Lana's body jerked forward at the sudden impact and her forehead cracked the steering wheel. A blast of pain rushed through her face and blood seeped to the surface of the cut. She moaned as she touched the slash upon her face and blood coated her fingertips. Her head was spinning wildly and her thoughts were clouded and confused.

Marty slammed on the brakes behind her and clamored out of his car. Booger followed.

"Holy shit!" he crowed. "Did you see that? That stupid spider plowed right into the jeep!"

"Was…that…Sp…Spence…or…Colette?" Booger asked as his face scrunched up and he darted to the edge of the precipice for a better look.

"No," Marty explained quickly as he immediately headed for the jeep and Lana who sat in a daze. "Spence is bigger and redder. That spider was black, black as night. And remember, Colette is smaller and is grayish to black with white stripes and orange and yellow spots."

"Yeah, yeah, yeah," Booger nodded his head exuberantly recalling how Colette had fought against Spence when he had taken her outside and wrestled her to the dirty ground. She was furious.

Then, when he took her cigarettes and stomped them into a mud puddle, she exploded in rage. Her eyes flared from red to black; and then, she transformed. She fought it at first, screaming as the limbs broke through her skin and her body mutated. He had thought she must have been in a lot of pain. But man, was that shit the bomb, he mused. Openly, he smiled.

"Do ya remember the look on Colette's face when she was transforming?" Marty asked Booger. "She was scared and pissed all at the same time. Man, that was priceless!" He chuckled; then turning his attention back to Lana, he swung his weight up on one arm and jumped up onto the back of the jeep.

Gripping the jeep keys tightly, Lana desperately swung at him.

"Come here, you." He grabbed her by the hair with his good hand and shielded her blows with his body. Yanking her head back, he stared into her face. "I wanna' taste your blood and see what all this black widow shit is all about. It looks pretty cool ta' me."

Lana trembled and her eyes were weighted with terror. "No," she begged in a whisper as Marty bent and gazed at her intently. His breath was upon her face as he studied the cut upon her forehead and his tongue slipped from between his narrow lips.

Suddenly, Evan flew up over the edge of the cliff. And, ramming into Marty, he sent him sailing nearly twenty-five feet away from the jeep.

Marty somersaulted backward and his injured shoulder slammed to the earth.

"*Oh, my God!*" he screamed. "*Oh, my God!*"

Booger raced toward him. "M…Mar…ty! Are… you…o…kay?"

Evan positioned himself between the two males and the jeep where Lana was. And, crouching in attack position, he waited for either to advance. Through his eight eyes, he watched as Booger pulled a large switchblade from his jacket pocket and flicked it open, while Marty writhed on the ground in pain.

"Evan?" Lana whispered. "Is that you?"

Two of Evan's eyes shot in her direction and he observed her from where he was crouched.

Booger suddenly advanced on him with his blade thrust forward. His hand shook along with his voice. "Y…you…mon…ster!" He ran in Evan's direction.

Evan dodged and immediately ejected the silken webbing from his spinnerets. In a matter of seconds, Booger was wrapped in the strands and wiggling upon the ground.

"D…damn…y…you!" His eyes burned with anger.

Evan stared at him now through all eight of his eyes. They flitted quietly; while the black marble-like pupils took in the whole of the situation. A mortal enemy was present and also the arachnid female. He would do anything to protect her. Plus, the animalistic thirst which blazed throughout his being desired fulfillment. He needed to feed; however, there was something else which ached within his bones. It wasn't the human's innards and blood that he craved so intensely. This was stronger; a burning surge of fire caused by what he now knew was Lana. He moved in her direction.

Lana turned to look at him. The haze slowly lifted from her mind and she blinked her eyes.

"Evan?" She knew it was him without even asking. Electricity steadily thrummed beneath her skin and blood stirred within her veins. The corners of her mouth puckered slightly and she couldn't help but smile inside as he slowly approached her. His eight long legs moved in perfect rhythm toward her with each one barely touching the ground.

Evan now stood before her, nearly touching her with the long legs that stretched before him. Webbing slowly curled from beneath him and gradually snaked along her calves and thighs. Goosebumps rose along her flesh.

Gently, the strands wrapped around her buttocks and waist, then along the silk of her top to her breast, then to the curve of her neck. Except for her head, she was now completely wrapped in his cocoon.

Lana held her breath. The feelings she felt as he touched her, even in his arachnid form, were electrifying, intense, almost painful; yet, they were soothing and warm, feelings of solace. She desired more, more of him.

"Evan, what are you doing?" she choked out in a whisper.

Carefully and gently, he pulled her from the jeep, drawing her securely beneath him, against the hardened shell of his thorax. The hardened shell thrummed and pulsed; it was a result of the arduous fight, and, from being near her.

Then, suddenly, he turned and darted through the trees in the direction of the cabin.

More than anything, Lana wanted to continue on this journey, the journey leading away from danger, to wherever Evan wanted to take her. She had lost everything, her parents, her brother, and even herself to being a creature, a black widow spider. However, somehow, Evan made her feel whole, like she was perhaps part of something—part of him.

But, what about Ches? she thought. She realized that they were racing at an incredible speed in the opposite direction of where Ches was fighting against Spence and Colette. The thought of Ches being alone and hurt was unbearable, he had only been fighting because of her.

"Evan, stop," she spoke to the hardened blackness where her cheek lay. She could hear his heart beating at an accelerated pace; he was excited, exhilarated. He may not listen, for he was now a beast, an arachnid that had taken a female who was at this time completely vulnerable, vulnerable to his animalistic desires, whether for food or for a mate. His pace didn't slow. Using his webbing, he careened through the air utilizing the tree tops to quicken his pace toward the cabin.

"Evan." There was a slight more edge to Lana's voice. "You have to stop. You have to go back and help Ches."

Evan sailed through the trees, by-passing two large evergreens. Then, all of a sudden, he dropped nearly fifty feet and skidded to the ground. For a moment, he stood absolutely still.

Lana had screamed the entire descent; and, when they hit the canopy floor, she stopped and caught her breath. Suddenly, she became irate.

"Are you trying to kill me?"

His eight eyes shifted uneasily as he ignored her and searched the trees and thick vegetation while the tone of the forest had abruptly changed from a thriving chatter of birds and animals to a quiet tomb-like remoteness. Evan stood like a statue, except for his eyes which ardently searched the area.

The forest floor was obscured from sight by a compilation of leaves, mounds of scraggly shrubs, and briar thickets which ran amuck. Several old locusts, once alive and vibrant, were now broken and aged, reduced to mere rotting logs awaiting their return to earth.

"What's wrong?" Lana asked as she twisted her head around to see. Two of Evan's eyes cut in her direction and she could feel his exoskeleton tense.

The wind had picked up slightly and streams of sunlight broke through the thick canopy overhead. It touched various parts of the forest, shifting as the wind changed direction. That's when Lana saw it; the patchwork of gleaming silver strands shooting through the trees and thick brush. It was Spence's webbing.

He had somehow constructed a wall that reached to the tips of the trees; and, it had been without her or Evan detecting it. They were completely surrounded.

Evan angrily tossed his head, aware that his own animalistic desires had distracted him, made the beast within him nearly crazy for Lana and now also vulnerable. He'd make sure it wouldn't happen again. Not ever.

"Evan?" Lana anxiously asked. She could also sense that Spence was nearby, hidden within the heavy brush. Her body automatically responded and despite the warmth of the cocoon, she trembled. Suddenly, the snugness and thrill of being encased in Evan's cocoon was gone. Instead, fear of being vulnerable to an attack for them both was predominant.

"Evan, release me. You can't fight with me here." She watched as his eight eyes darted frantically in several directions; they flashed crimson to black, then back to crimson again. For Lana it was dizzying, almost like trying to focus on the flashing lights of a disco ball.

"Evan?"

Whether he was in human form or arachnid form, Evan's main concern would be to protect Lana. She was the female black widow; she was priority. His animalistic instincts were intensifying, increasing in power and strength. The thought of escaping to keep her safe was foremost in his mind.

Using all his force, he sprung high into the air

attempting to escape the wall of sticky threading that encased the perimeter and to utilize the cover of the trees. Easily clearing the wall, he raced in the direction of the river.

Spence bound into the air after them. However, his aerodynamic abilities weren't as skilled as Evan's and he was unable to get high enough. He sailed through the air, miscalculated, and headed in the direction of his own webbing. Quickly grasping onto a nearby branch, he spun around and awkwardly landed on the ground. A high-pitched screech ripped from his throat and he shook his head. Anger boiled through his beastly form and he fumed at the idea of having to double back around his own webbing to catch them.

Booger's hand still held the knife that he had pulled on Evan. It was pressed tightly against his side, constricted by the webbing that he was wrapped in. Slowly, he shifted it to where he could grip it firmly in his hand; then, he began the tedious task of slicing through one strand after another to free himself from the cocoon.

Time passed and he was finally free; and, brushing the severed strands from his body, he staggered to his feet. He searched the grassy area where his friend had previously landed when he was struck by Evan. "Mar…ty!" Then, he ran toward Ches's jeep that sat near the cliff's edge. "Mar…ty!"

Marty was slumped against the vehicle's hulking tire. The color had drained from his face giving him a ghostly, milk-white appearance and crimson rings rimmed his eyes. Booger was certain Marty had been crying.

"Mar…ty? Are...you...okay?" Booger hurried to his friend and knelt beside him.

Marty angrily ran his good arm across his face. "I can't move my left arm." He smirked. "Stupid spider got me good."

"I…hate…that…Ev…an! I…wish…he…were…dead!" Booger yelled.

"Yeah, me too," Marty agreed. His raspy chuckle at his friend's response caused him to wince in pain. Marty then glanced back at the jeep. "Hey," he asked in a cracked voice, "are the keys in the ignition?"

Booger stood and looked inside the vehicle; he didn't see the keys anywhere, though he did notice a fresh smear of blood on the steering wheel. His mind abruptly ran amuck with the idea of *him* having enough power and strength to defeat Evan and having the girl to himself.

"No…, Marty, the…keys…aren't…here." The corners of Booger's mouth then turned up in an impious grin and his eyes glinted in pleasure. Quickly, he swiped his index finger across the blood staining the steering wheel and stuck it in his mouth.

Chapter 3

Trey drove at top speed along the route that ran south toward Haim River. Then, he turned left onto the dirt road that ran parallel to the water. He scanned the area watching for any sign of Ches, hoping that he wasn't too late.

"Damn, Ches, I knew this was trouble," he growled beneath his breath. A bad feeling stirred within his stomach and he pressed on the gas. Suddenly, he stopped the car. "*Holy shit*," slipped from his breath.

Blood colored the dusty road, as if a large animal had been struck by a vehicle and drug into the weeds.

Trey hurriedly turned off the car, jumped out and slung the gun over his shoulder. His heart pounded in his chest as he darted from one side of the road to another searching for anything that would indicate what had happened. Suddenly, he saw Ches's knife lying by the edge of the road.

"Ches…Ches! Damn it!" he shouted. Then, running back to the car, he reached in through the open window and blew the horn. "Ches!"

The ray's of the noonday sun were streaming through the broken area of forest and careening off the chrome of the Charger. That's when Trey noticed the silver streaks of webbing gleaming within the trees. He ran in that direction, terrified of what he might find.

Trey slammed to a halt—shocked at what he saw.

An enormous cocoon was suspended high up in the sprawling trunk of a large oak tree. It was nearly the size of a coffin.

Trey stared at it in disbelief. “Oh, my God. What is that?” Slowly, he stepped forward, his heart sinking as he immediately imagined the worse.

“Ches?” He quickly grabbed a long branch that was lying on the ground, snapped the spindly branches from it, then reached up and touched the cocoon. The webbing was sturdy, yet the outer surface was sticky and clung to the tree branch like cotton candy.

“Oh my God!” He tossed the stick as his mind raced through the various fishing items that remained in the trunk of the car.

In several quick strides, he was back at the Charger. His hands trembled as he reached into his jeans pockets and removed his keys. “Damn it! Quit shaking!”

Sticking the key into the lock, he flung the trunk lid open. Then, he hurriedly rummaged through the items scattered around inside: fishing rods, collapsible chairs, an expandable net and a collection of filleting knives. He cursed again.

“Why couldn’t this have been whaling season, or apple picking season? At least I’da had a harpoon or a ladder, or something!”

He grabbed one of the small chairs, the net and a few filleting knives. And, though the knives were small, they would come in handy for cutting through the webbing. Tossing them in a pack that had been amongst the fishing gear, he shouldered his collection and headed back toward the area where the cocoon was hanging. Hurriedly removing the chair and the gun from his shoulder, he positioned the chair on the ground just beneath the cocoon and quickly propped the rifle against the tree.

"If you're in there, Ches, don't worry, I'm getting you out."

Carefully, he straddled the chair, while being extra cautious not to concentrate too much weight on the wooden base or the canvas seat. And, though he was nearly six foot, 191 pounds, the chair should hold for at least a few minutes… he hoped.

Reaching up, he sliced through the strands securing the cocoon at the top. Webbing stuck to his jeans and t-shirt. It was inches from his face. And, though it was mostly odorless, it contained a mild earthy smell and the consistency made you think of cotton-candy.

The heavy mass suddenly slumped forward, making it easier to pry the upper portion loose. However, as his weight shifted, so did the chair.

"Holy sh…!"He scrambled wildly to hang on. And, with the additional weight, the wood of the chair cracked and splintered beneath his feet.

Trey grabbed at the cocoon; and for a brief moment, he was hanging from it and the tree.

"Whoa! Hang on Trey!" he shouted to himself.

Suddenly, the strands of webbing broke and he and the cocoon careened backward and hit the ground.

"Ugh!" The air whooshed from his lungs as the heavy cocoon landed on top of him. Rolling the cocoon off, he struggled to catch a breath.

"Oh my God," he finally breathed as he stared blankly up at the sky. His distorted mind drifted to a time when he and Ches had been wrestling and Ches had jumped on him from the stairs sending him crashing to the living room floor and squashing Trey like a bug.

His mind gradually came into focus. "Ches?"

Trey clambered to his feet and shook his head. Still slightly dizzy, he glanced around in search of the knives, thinking it was fortunate he hadn't fallen on one.

Seeing one, he quickly grabbed it. Then, turning his attention back to the cocoon, he dropped to his knees and went to work cutting away at the strands.

Sweat beaded his forehead and his body ached from the fall.

"Aw, man, Ches—I hope I'm wrong and you're not in here." His hand mildly shook as he sliced through the crown of the cocoon. The webbing stuck to his hands, the blade of the knife and his clothing.

He wondered how Ches had cut *him* free from the webbing that Evan had secured him in, when they had fought on the roof. Evan had allowed him to live by leaving his face uncovered so that he could breathe. So, he had returned the favor by saving him from Spence.

However, Ches may not be so lucky, *if* this enormous monstrosity was him.

Trey sliced through the webbing faster, as if he were expertly filleting a fish. The deeper he cut, the more frequent claret coloring strands appeared within the bundle of gray-white and the more pliant they became. Panic scraped his nerves and he ground his teeth. He had to go faster.

"Ches?" He could now see several strands of blonde hair, some stained with blood. He stared in disbelief.

"Ches! This can't be you. I have to be wrong!"

Tossing the knife, he tore at the webbing with his bare hands.

"Ches!"

The threads were strong, like pulling on fishing line. They tore at his hands as he gripped each one and pulled with all his might. His hands began to bleed.

Frantically, he dug through each layer uncovering Ches's face, head and neck. Suddenly, his breath caught in his throat at what he saw.

All natural coloring was drained from Ches's skin, and was replaced by a sickly blue-green, plum-colored shadow, like the distorted shades of a severe bruise. Numerous bite marks covered his neck and ran deep, puckering black around each hole. Trey mentally counted twelve.

"Ches?" His voice quavered as he patted his friend's cheek. "Ches, come on!" His hands shook as he pressed his two fingers to an uninjured area upon his neck and felt for a pulse. There was nothing.

Grabbing the knife again, he rapidly cut through the top layer of strands covering Ches's chest, then he tore away at the rest. His mind raced with each passing second while he couldn't seem to be able to tear through the layers fast enough.

"Come on! Come on!" he breathed. Sweat beaded his body as he ripped through the last layer and immediately began to administer CPR. "One, two, three, breathe. One, two, three… breathe. Come on, buddy. Breathe!" Exhaling, he placed his fingers to Ches's neck again.

"Damn you, Ches! Fight back!" Tears sprang to the back of his eyes and he struggled against their coming. He pressed on Ches's chest harder. "Fight back! You never let anyone beat you before! Don't start now!"

Suddenly a snickering cough came from within the thick brush just a few yards away. Trey scrambled over to the gun and immediately spun to crouch on one knee.

"Who's out there?" he angrily shouted while brushing an arm across his wet eyes. He pointed the rifle in the direction from where the sound came. "Show yourself!"

Colette slipped from behind a large hemlock and leaned against it for support. Her back was slightly hunched and she looked disheveled, like a cat that had been fighting or whipped through a fan. Her clothing was tattered and her normally pale skin was now white.

Trey immediately noticed the three partially severed spider legs hanging limply from her back and the hourglass marking on her torso that was somewhat similar to Lana's. He quickly stood to his feet.

Colette's fiery scarlet hair was wild and tangled and stood up on her head matching the crimson color of her flashing eyes, which reverted from red to black. Blood spattered her front and caked a large incision running from her hairline to her left brow and she seemed to be in pain; however, she snickered again in spite of it.

Then, she parted her flaming red lips and licked a spatter of blood at the corner of her mouth. Her eyes darted from Ches then back to Trey as hunger plagued her gaze and a peculiar look riddled her face. She snidely remarked, "You can't bring him back you know. His body was poisoned, then sucked dry of fluids."

Her high-pitched, nasally voice scraped irritably along Trey's skin and he shook his head fighting the morbid images that entered his mind. He weakly dropped to his knees as vomit broke at the back of his throat and he had to swallow to hold it back.

If maybe I'da gotten here sooner or possibly gone with him, he thought. Why *did I let him go alone; we* never *went alone*. Grief consumed him and he wanted to lash out, break free of its indescribable pain which was tearing at his chest.

"No, he *will* come back," he stated desperately as tears now streamed his cheeks. "He's not dead!"

Colette snickered and her lips quivered as she spoke. "It was our first feeding. We were both starving."

Trey's body shook with rage as he balled his fists and stared at her through burning eyes. His words came through strained measured breaths. "*You* did this with Spence? *You*?"

"Well, yes." She lavishly licked her lips. "And, he tasted good." Her eyes sparked with life and that same peculiar look crossed her face, like she was awaiting a meal—waiting to feed.

Trey had heard enough. He didn't want to shoot her, he wanted to beat her, beat her to a bloody pulp. Laying down the gun, he sprang.

"*Damn you, you witch!*" Slamming into Colette, he sent her stumbling backward. However, she quickly recovered and settled into a crouched position. And, though she was badly injured, her strength and speed was a hundred times that of a normal human. He fought vehemently, while his heart ached and rage became an unbearable beast within him: He had to beat her.

Colette threw her fists and kicked her bare feet like a professional fighter, and threading began to stream from the marking over her navel. Using this to his advantage, Trey grabbed several strands and yanked her toward him. Then, he reached around and snatched one of the several legs and angrily twisted it.

She cried out in pain.

"I'll kill you!" he shouted. Then, he spun her around and secured his arm around her throat. His forearm bulged and flexed as she struggled and he listened to her gasp for air. He wanted to crush her windpipe, or snap her neck, make her feel a minute amount of pain that Ches had felt. But, that wouldn't be enough; it probably wouldn't even kill her. Plus, he wanted Spence's neck too.

"Where's Spence?" he breathed into her ear.

"I don't know."

He tightened his grip. "Yes you do. Now, tell me! Where is Spence?"

Colette gagged and her head twitched. And, thinking he may be actually killing her, he released the pressure on her throat slightly so she could answer.

Suddenly, she sprang upward; and, abruptly throwing her head back, she cracked him square in the face. It was like being hit in the face with a bowling ball. Blood burst from his nose and mouth and he momentarily lost his hold. Then, Colette rapidly spun around and kicked him in the groin.

Trey doubled-over and dropped to one knee. He desperately needed to catch a breath as a lightning bolt of pain raced through his stomach to meet the excruciating pain in his face. He shook his head in an attempt to remain conscious.

The gurgling sound of his own blood began to form in his ears and he placed a hand to his face. He knew his nose was broken.

Unable to feel his lips which were saturated in a river of blood, he knew she now had the upper hand. Momentarily, he wondered if this is what it had been like for Ches.

Trey watched through a clouded vision as Colette circled him like a lioness ready to attack its prey. Hunger burned in her crimson eyes, which were now hard as diamonds, while her passing stare clung to his bleeding face. She relished in each drop of bright red blood that landed on the ground before him and licked her lips in anticipation.

"What are you waiting for?" Trey choked out as his heart banged in his chest and his head spun. "Go ahead, suck me dry."

Chapter 4

Evan moved rapidly through one tree top to another, barely touching a one as he sailed through the air and easily scaled the raging river. He crossed the water trying to lose Spence, but also in an attempt to get Lana away from the situation.

"Evan, what are you gonna do?"

Webbing shot from the spinnerets lining both sides of where she was being held against his thorax. All of a sudden, they touched down on a bulky branch of a sycamore tree. Evan's eight eyes, flashing scarlet to black, darted in every direction and Lana had to close her eyes to keep from becoming dizzy. She briefly wondered whether or not she would be able to use her power of persuasion on him while he was a beast. She might possibly have to try if he wouldn't listen to her and go back to where Ches was. Opening her eyes, she looked directly at him.

"Evan, we have to go back. We have to make sure Ches is okay." He shook his large head, averting his gaze from the forest to her and staring at her with all eight eyes. A slight breeze was blowing, rustling the trees and the tiny hairs covering his body. She looked at him, wondering if he was able to understand her, comprehend the human words that she spoke. All eight pupils were fixed on her; no longer flashing from crimson to black, they remained motionless, perfect onyx marbles set deep within the beast's skull, each covered with a clear shell.

"Evan, please. Ches was bringing me to find you." Lana focused on the tone of her voice, being as gentle and alluring as possible while also deciding she would attempt to persuade him into listening to her by using the power she possessed with her eyes.

"*Please*."

He continued to stare and she wondered if her power to control him was working. The energy within her seeped from her to him; however, she knew now what she was doing. It wasn't just a roller coaster ride her emotions were on; it was the beast within her aiming to take control. Trembling slightly, she continued to look sternly into his eyes and remain firm.

Evan slowly opened his mouth and his jagged fangs emerged. They were just inches from her face. His breath was warm upon her skin as he released a low hiss.

"Evan, I know you can understand me." His huge body pressed firmly against her as a droplet of golden liquid seeped from each fang. "We have to go back."

The weight of him increased as he bent his legs and was nearly lying on top of her.

"Evan, you're too heavy, you're crushing me." Besides being somewhat frightened, she was becoming a bit irate. She tried adamantly to break free.

"Now, stop this," she stated firmly as her eyes

blazed from deep mahogany to black. The arachnid beast within her was also becoming irate. "You stop this right now."

Immediately, he stopped pressing against her and slowly pulled away. He stood erect on all eight legs, tilted his head, and stared at her.

Drawing at a much needed breath, Lana then attempted once more to persuade him into turning around. And, though she was still slightly irritated, her voice shook faintly as she tried again.

"Evan, please. Listen to me."

Hissing loudly, he tossed his head from side to side. And, though he was in his arachnid form, an irrepressible beast controlled only by natural instinct, he acknowledged every word she said. And, realizing that if he didn't do something and Ches was killed, Lana would never forget it.

Evan's fangs disappeared as he angrily sprang from the tree and headed back in the direction from which they just came.

Trey's mind raced through his options as the blood streamed from his nose and his vision was blurred. Colette was now just a distorted figure before him, a mechanical rag doll swaying methodically to a silent note. He grasped for a breath and coughed as blood ran down his throat.

"I know what it is; you have to transform into that

beast to drain me dry." He fought the fear that was rising in his gut. "And, you hate that hideous beast, hate the way it looks and hate the way it smells. It's ugly!" he shouted at her. "So, that makes *you* ugly!"

Her body froze and rage flared in her crimson eyes. "What do you know about it?" she screeched.

"Because, you are now revolting, a warped creature that will never be attractive again to anyone."

"Shut up!" she snapped. "I'll kill you *without* turning!"

"You can't." He swiped the sweat and blood from his face. "Because the repugnant monster that's burning inside you wants my blood and wants to feed." His head dropped and he slipped to all fours. "So, go ahead, Colette, transform and feed that hideous beast within you."

"I won't!" she fumed. "I won't let it control me!" Fury sent her into a maddened frenzy and strands of webbing began to ooze uncontrollably from the hourglass marking over her navel.

Her gaze quickly shot to her stomach and she screamed in rage.

"Look! Look what you've done!" she screeched as the five remaining, undamaged, legs tore through the skin on her back. Painfully, she cried out as she dropped to her knees and the transformation quickly consumed her.

Remembering the gun lying beneath the tree, Trey immediately sprang in that direction. Within five swift strides he reached the weapon and clutched it in his hand.

However, Colette was now in her arachnid form. She was quick and powerful and immediately, pounced on his back. Her fangs dug deep within his shoulder making him blind with excruciating pain. They pumped and thrummed, buried within his skin, and poison was quickly being injected into his body. He immediately felt sick.

Crying out, he swung his fist back in an uppercut to her forehead. And, as her fangs briefly ripped from his skin, he spun around and unloaded the gun into her face.

Lana flinched with each roaring gunshot that echoed though the forest and thundered within her ears. Then, frantically glancing up at Evan who had also heard them, she conveyed with the urgency in her eyes what he needed to do.

Evan increased his speed and raced in that direction, the direction where Ches had been fighting Spence and Colette. They would be there in a matter of minutes.

Diana spun around in her saddle at the sound of the gunshots discharging on her parent's property. Then, heeling Sarge, her horse, she galloped in that direction.

She had been out riding attempting to clear her thoughts and emotions, rid herself of the severe pain she felt because of Evan. She cursed as she thought of Lana, blaming her for Evan's behavior. However, right now, someone was shooting on her property and she wanted to find out who and why.

Diana's hand slipped to her saddlebag where she now carried her father's 357 Magnum. *The hell with fighting*, she thought, *too easy to get damaged, ruin my beauty.* She touched the side of her face where her bruise from Spence had been, just grateful she hadn't lost any of her perfect teeth. *No, next time I'll just shoot the bastard.*

As an expert rider, she rode hard and fast, rapidly dodging the trees of the forest like an experienced barrel racer. Sarge's inhaling and exhaling spurts of breath matched the rhythm of his stride. She pushed him even harder.

Bursting through an opening in the trees, he leapt out onto the dirt road then slowed to a stop. Diana pulled his reigns to the right and clicked her tongue. Then, pressing her heels to his side, they headed south along the dirt road. A cloud of dust rose behind them.

Trey's head spun and he suddenly toppled backward to the ground. The poison Colette had injected into him was rushing through his veins at lightning speed and he could feel the pain exploding within his arteries, snaking through his system like a rattler through brush. Excruciating pain raced to every extremity it seeped to. And, turning his head to the side, he vomited.

He could see Colette's immense form from where he lay. The shots from the rifle had completely removed her head. No wonder he liked that gun so much… it did the job. Rolling to his side, he clutched at his stomach. "Oh my God," he breathed. And, as white hot pain rushed to his head, he cried out.

"Whoa," Diana called to Sarge the minute she saw the black charger sitting ahead in the distance. Briefly, she observed the car from where she was. Then, clicking her tongue, she heeled the horse and hurried in that direction.

Shouting the command again, they came to a screeching halt. Diana quickly dismounted.

A trail of blood was staining the road, leading into the nearby forest. She thought it might be an injured deer or an animal that may have been attacked, until she heard someone moan.

Leading Sarge to a nearby locust tree, she secured his reigns and observed the area. The air was still, too quiet for her liking, and not a single bit of nature was stirring.

Something was seriously wrong.

Unbinding the leather strap to the saddlebag, she reached inside and removed the 357 Magnum. Her heart thumped uncontrollably beneath her shirt and sweat broke upon her brow. Quietly and cautiously, she moved through the thick brush and trees, her eyes scanning the area like a prowling cat. She headed in the direction of the person's cries. Then, inhaling deep, she burst through the trees.

"Oh my God!" the words screamed from her throat at what she saw.

Blood covered nearly every inch of the forest's floor, including the young man that lay helplessly in the center of the clearing. Beside him was a freakish looking creature, like that of a giant spider whose bloody head lay just feet away. The odor of death was atrocious, gagging. A thousand thoughts surged through her mind as her head spun and she grasped at a tree to steady herself. Then, quickly turning, she attempted to fight the abrupt nausea that roiled in her stomach while her breaths were measured and deep.

Bending, Diana took a breath. And, that's when she noticed the large cocoon torn open and lying on the ground.

"Oh my God." She stepped closer, to see the mangled person inside.

"What in Heaven's name happened here?"

Immediately, she cursed for not having her cell phone. And, thinking that even if she galloped Sarge at top speed for help, it would probably be too late.

Her legs, now compared to cooked pasta, wobbled as she slowly stepped in Trey's direction. "Hello?"

The only response was a low hollow groan, the sound of someone who was rapidly dying. Diana moved closer, all the while attempting to avoid the massive amounts of blood soaking the forest floor.

Trey's eyes were closed as she dropped to her knees beside him and tried to assess the damage done to his body. Her hand shook as she laid the gun down and gently touched him on the shoulder. The smell of vomit was choking her throat.

Swallowing hard, she asked, "Hello? Can ya'll hear me?"

Slowly, Trey opened his eyes which were now dark, hollow sockets, lost of all their original color and spark.

A meek smile crossed Diana's quavering lips while the last thing she felt like doing was smiling. Her threaded emotions appeared in her quaking words as she asked, "Is there anythin' I can do?" Quickly assessing his wounds, her eyes paused on the two extensive gouges in his back.

His reply was barely a whisper, "Ches…" His eyes slowly closed and he gasped for a single breath.

"What?" Diana's accent spiked as she moved her ear closer to his face. "What did ya'll say?"

Chapter 5

Spotting Diana's horse and Trey's car, Evan slightly averted his course by sailing through the air and careening left. He landed in a secluded spot just a few yards from where the fight had been and rapidly began to tear away at Lana's cocoon with his teeth. Lana slipped from within the strands and gently dropped to her haunches on the ground.

Quickly brushing the loose strands of webbing from her clothes, she glanced at Evan who just stared back. Briefly touching his head, she said, "Thank you." Then, turning, she hurriedly ran in the direction where she could sense Ches.

The various odors of blood were thick in the air, a blanket of soil upon her nostrils and skin; one of them was his. She was mildly surprised at how good it smelled. Then, she heard Diana's voice.

"Ches?" Lana called out, only to hear a reply from Diana.

"Over here!" Diana replied.

Lana didn't have the time to question Diana's presence; she had to find Ches. And, terrified of what she might find, she burst through the last row of trees. Then, she froze.

"Oh my God!" Her eyes frantically raced to Colette's dead body, then shot to see Trey lying on the ground before Diana.

"What are ya'll doin' here?" Diana snapped.

Lana ignored her remark.

"Trey! Oh my God, what happened?" Hurrying to his side, she dropped to her knees. Then, she looked at Diana and yelled, "Where's Ches?"

"Are ya'll referrin' to that guy over there?"

Lana immediately followed her pointing finger. A large cocoon lay on the ground several yards away and she could just barely make out Ches's features from where she was.

"No!" Lana cried. "No!" Stumbling to her feet, she ran to where he was lying in the cocoon. "Ches!"

Slipping to the ground, she reached within the cocoon and pulled him toward her. Tears stained her cheeks as she held him tightly and sobbed. "Ches, I'm sorry. I'm so sorry." She pushed a few blonde curls away from his face. Then, she looked for Evan, hoping he would help.

Evan stepped into the open, wrapped only in the navy and gray plaid saddle blanket he had taken from Diana's horse. It was cinched around his waist and his hair stood straight on his head. His dark eyes were flashing from black to various hues of red and mahogany. He looked slightly crazed.

"Evan?" Diana spun on her knees. She caught herself wanting to go to him, but quickly thought better of it. His narrowed gaze was painfully watching Lana, and sadness veiled his face. Diana hated the situation.

Evan turned his attention toward her and then to Trey. The adverse circumstances had suddenly become worse with Diana present. His senses then abruptly averted to all the blood that was saturating his nose, nearly causing him to want to transform back and feed. Quickly, he had to get himself in check.

"Evan, we have to do something!" Lana's cry broke the awkward silence. "Please!"

"What's goin' on here, Evan?" Diana stood to her feet. Clenching her hands to her hips, she eyed them through an icy stare.

"Ya'll don't seem very surprised by that there monster that's lying over there with its head blown completely off! And, how, and why, are ya'll out here? Am I missin' somethin'?"

Evan slipped past Diana and quickly dropped to his knees to examine Trey. "I can't do anything with Diana here," his words were directed to Lana. "She's going to have to leave."

Diana's gaze cut to him and then to Lana. Thunder clouds of rage suddenly covered her face. Stomping her foot, she angrily replied, "No! I'm not leavin' Evan! Somethin' huge is goin' on here and I wanna' know about it. Besides, this here is *my* property!"

Evan's shoulders dropped and he gave in to her tantrum. "Okay, then suit yourself; but, you're not gonna' like what you see. Now, is this your father's gun?" He picked up the weapon she had laid beside her and quickly examined it."

"Yes. Yes it is," she replied.

"I assume it's loaded."

She nodded her head.

"Well, then stand as far over there as you can." He pointed to a spot about twenty feet away between two trees; then, he handed her the gun. "And, if you see anything bigger than a rabbit heading in our direction, shoot it—don't hesitate—just shoot it." He turned his attention back to Trey; then, remembering something else, he spun around to glance at her. "Oh, and…don't look at me."

Diana cocked her head to the side, and for a brief moment, she stood firm, unwilling to budge. Then, suddenly turning, she stomped in the direction Evan had pointed.

"And, Lana," His expression was stone, unreadable, as he looked over at her tear streaked face, "from what Grandmother Hobbs' had once told me, I think you can help Ches. But, you know, he'll never be the same."

Briefly, he glanced down at his own hands wondering, if *he* would have had the choice of being brought back to life as an arachnid—a hideous beast—versus death, which would he have chosen? He then turned his attention back to Lana.

"You'll have to transform completely and bite him, retract all the venom, and then send all the blood you can into him. You're the only one who can do it, because you're a female black widow, and it's only possible with a female. However, a word of warning… if you bite him and get hungry, or send any of your venom into him, he will remain dead." Evan took a breath and added, "Also, you may wanna' undress first; that's a nice outfit and it will definitely get ruined."

Lana's mouth dropped open and the color rushed from her face. "I don't know if I can," she stammered.

Evan looked at her. "What—transform, or undress?"

She answered grimly, "Both."

"Well, if you want him alive bad enough, you'll do it. I can't. I can only withdraw the venom. So, I can help Trey; but, I can *not* help Ches."

Evan took one last look at Lana, glanced over at Diana to make sure her back was to him, then began to transform.

Hearing Evan groan, Diana readily spun around to watch. She clutched at her chest as the blanket fell away from him and the eight legs, tearing through the skin on his back, grew long and unruly. He grimaced in pain with each segment of his body that changed from his head to his feet.

She couldn't help but cry out, "What's happening to him?"

Lana didn't answer, but also watched in mild trepidation as Evan continued to transform and change into the black widow spider. He stood as a mammoth over Trey's unmoving body, enormous and black, a huge beast. A look of hunger plagued his crimson eyes.

"Evan?" Lana called his name in fear that his

animal instinct would take over and he wouldn't help Trey, but destroy him. His gazed darted to meet hers as he ran his elongated feelers along Trey's body like two antennas bending to search for reception. Then, without any warning, he opened his mouth and sunk his enormous fangs deep into Trey's kidney.

Lana flinched as Trey arched upward and cried out in excruciating pain. His body writhed and he fought feebly in an attempt to stave Evan off.

"Evan! Stop!" Lana cried after a few moments. "Stop! You're killing him!"

Diana was froze. And, unable to stand Trey's screaming any longer, she placed her hands over her ears. "Evan honey, stop. Please stop!" Tears raced from her eyes and lined her cheeks. She thought she might faint.

Suddenly, Evan dropped Trey, and quickly turning, hissed at Lana. Blood dripped from his exposed fangs and he released an assemblage of ear piercing screeches. Then, after several moments, his body began to change and he transformed back into himself. He looked wilder, more animalistic than he had previously and his eyes burned as roaring flames.

Grabbing the blanket, he briefly looked at Lana then Diana; then turning on his heels, he walked into the trees. He needed a moment to clear his head. For the few droplets he had ingested of Trey's blood had tasted good, good enough for him to want to drain him dry. It forced him to struggle against the urge for more.

And, with the knowledge boring into his subconscious that he would be involved in changing Ches into a beast, he needed a moment of redemption from his sin. Plus, Diana now knew he and Lana's secret. That made things even worse.

Diana and Lana watched as Evan made his way into the forest and disappeared. "Where's he goin'?" Diana asked no one in particular.

Lana just stared after him suddenly realizing that this wasn't what he wanted—to become a beast, become something unnatural and inhuman that sought to feed on others. What he wanted was a normal life, a quiet life, exactly what he didn't have. Her heart ached for him and she wanted to go to him, surround him with all the love he needed to put his mind at ease. However, right now, there were more pressing issues at hand; and, saving Ches from the darkness his body and soul were subjected to, was it.

She was unsure how she felt about Heaven and Hell. Ches's death must have been a living hell, excruciatingly painful and torturous like the deepest darkest crevasses of an eternal nightmare. And, being the only one who could possibly save him, she needed to remain strong.

"Ches," she whispered into his ear. "I'll bring you back. I promise." Placing a kiss upon his cheek, she then stood to her feet.

Diana shot an irate glance in her direction, "Don't

tell me ya'll are gonna' do that too."

Lana nodded her head and her eyes locked with Diana's. Then, she began to undress.

Slowly, she removed the burgundy top; then, she gently folded it and laid it on the grass beside her. Her body felt mechanical, like a marionette played by a string and her fingers felt numb as she tugged at the belted waistband of the skirt. Sliding it down her legs, she gingerly stepped from inside it, folded it and laid it with the other garment. A cool breeze ran along her skin and her body shivered. Then, she removed her undergarments and laid them with the other pieces of clothing.

Diana suddenly snapped her open jaw closed with the realization she had been staring. Anger thundered across her face and she rolled her eyes toward Heaven.

"Holy cow bells, Lana, I've already seen ya'll; so, why didn't ya'll wait until I turned around?" Diana's blonde hair whipped and her arms crossed as she flippantly spun to face the forest.

Lana briefly stood there watching Diana, suddenly realizing that she no longer felt intimidated or menial compared to her, or any other human being for that matter. Her mind-set was becoming focused, strengthened as she, without hesitation, closed her eyes and concentrated on the black widow within her and the scented bouquet of blood surrounding her. Briefly, her mind and body struggled as the hate for what she had become immediately crept into her thoughts and momentarily broke her concentration. It nearly sent her pitching forward and she quickly planted her feet to remain upright.

A river of tears reflexively streamed her cheeks as her body subconsciously fought against the beast, fought the change she was going through, and against the desire to feed, or kill.

"*Nnnooooo!*" she cried out as webbing poured from the mark upon her abdomen and snaked along her body. It fought to consume her, wrap her in the webbed cocoon; however, she stood firm and unyielding. And squeezing her eyes tight, she raised her arms as the webbing snaked around her legs and torso and continued upward toward her chest and neck. Venom, hot as molten lava, poured through her pumping veins racing through her body at a tremendous speed and she was becoming stronger, faster, more agile and suddenly hungry. Her respiratory system and organs instantly expanded and her eyes jerked open in terror as suddenly her ribs cracked and she could no longer breathe. She began to struggle, fight for a breath as the webbing instantly responded and snaked along her neck and chin.

Evan was watching from a distance, spellbound by her transformation. However, his body quickly reacted as her bones snapped and he could no longer hear her breathing. Bolting from within the trees, he raced toward her.

"Lana! No! Don't do it!"

Her eyes closed and her head slumped to her chest.

"Lana!" Evan reached out to grab her from falling forward, when suddenly her eyes flew open and she strangely cocked her head. Her irises were two pits of fiery crimson, blazing from red to black, then back to red again. Bewilderment flashed in their wild stare and Evan came to a screeching halt. He took a step backward.

"Lana?"

The webbing completely consumed her and Evan stood dumbfounded as to what to do. His first several transformations had been different, while taking hour after painful hour to complete. He wondered if hers would be the same.

A few moments passed as he and Diana just stared. Then, suddenly, the cocoon burst open and Lana appeared, though not as herself, but as the black widow female.

Diana gasped, unable to believe her eyes. And, again, she had to steady herself while wondering when she would awake from this horrific nightmare.

Lana's eight eyes darted in every direction and she seemed bewildered, like a newborn child subjected to a new, terrifying world.

Evan cautiously stepped toward her. "Lana?" Suddenly, her bewildered gaze snapped and all eight of her eyes flashed with rage. A hair-raising screech tore from her throat and she abruptly stiffened and crouched into an attack position.

"Evan! Git away from her! She looks like she's gonna' attack!" Diana cried.

Lana's gaze cut from Evan to Diana then back to Evan again. She was a massive beast, powerful and strong, yet agile and fast. Her front legs thrashed out at Evan and he hurriedly dodged out of their way and ducked into the trees.

"Diana, run!" he yelled as he circled around and ran in her direction.

Diana's body was frozen in place as she watched Lana quickly scurry across the terrain in her direction with her mouth open and her fangs bared. Finding her voice, she screamed and turned to run. Lana snapped at her, just catching the back of her shirt.

"Oh my God!" Diana's heart banged in her chest and she stumbled forward trying to find a large enough tree to hide behind—Lana was enormous.

"Lana!" Evan pushed Diana out of the way as Lana attempted at another bite. "Lana! Stop! You can't let it control you! You have to help Ches! Think of Ches!" His heart ached at the words he shouted, ached terribly; but, somehow he needed to stop her. And, even if he did transform, he was a male and she was a female: He would never be able to physically take her. It may end up killing them both if he tried. "Lana!"

Lana looked at the two people before her while the hunger inside her ravaged her thoughts, stole any human control she had.

"Evan, help me," her inner self silently cried out as

she desperately fought the creature, fought the control it now had over her and the thirst that was consuming her.

"Help me! I can't stop!"

Webbing shot in Evan's direction and Lana speedily worked to wrap him and draw him to her.

"Nnoooooo!" her human mind cried out. Her razor sharp fangs burst from her mouth. They were dripping with venom.

Two gunshots suddenly rang out and Lana stumbled backward and into the trees. Her flaring gaze cut to Diana as she immediately dropped Evan and screeched out in excruciating pain. Then, tilting forward, her immense body thudded to the ground.

Diana shook as the smoking gun slipped from her hands. "I won't let ya'll kill him! I won't!" Then, surging forward on trembling legs, she ran to help Evan.

Chapter 6

Fearing he would hurt Marty if he moved him, Booger hollered out in hopes of having Spence hear.

"Spence!" The sound of his imperfect voice echoed through the trees and foliage, heightening the clicking made with each word.

"Spence…where…are…you?"

"Maybe he ran into some trouble." Marty's voice was rough, strained, while his entire side burned in pain. "Maybe you should go look for him and Colette."

Booger glanced at his good friend and nodded his head. "I'll…be…right…back. You…stay…right…here."

After being unable to find Evan, Spence had doubled back in hopes of locating the others and regrouping. Utilizing his webbing, he quickly headed in the direction of where he and Colette had fed on Ches, and then separated.

He had been satisfied with Colette's performance as a black widow; now, he had plans for them both. However, the millions of miniscule hairs on his body perked to alertness. It was the sound of gunshots in the far-off distance.

Diana had hurried to find something to cut the strands encasing Evan. Locating one of the filleting knives, she quickly cut him free.

"Were ya'll just gonna' let her suck ya' dry?" she hollered at him as she tore the strands from his face. "What the heck's the matter with ya'll, Evan Labonte?"

"What happened?" he asked confused. "Where's Lana?" Tearing the webbing away with his hands, he awkwardly climbed to his feet. "What happened?" he questioned her again, while rubbing his head with his hand.

Diana looked at him incredulously, "Are ya'll serious, ya' don't remember?"

Evan cocked his head then glanced around to see Lana's transformed figure lying on the ground. Blood oozed from the bullet holes in her head and her immense body labored for breaths.

"What the hell happened?" He ran to her and dropped to his knees. "Who shot her?"

"Well…Diana hesitated. Then, enraged by the situation and from being attacked, she angrily stated, "I did! That stupid girl was tryin' ta eat ya'll, so I shot 'er. There! That's all there is to it. I shot 'er!"

Evan's eyes turned black and he angrily snapped at her. "Don't you ever hurt her again, Diana."

The color drained from her face and she quickly turned her head.

Evan averted his attention from her back to Lana

whose body was rapidly beginning to transform back into her human state.

"Come on; help me get these three into Trey's car. Spence could return any minute." He scooped Lana up into his arms.

Diana spun. She was hurt and wanted to retaliate—retaliate against Evan for rejecting her, and retaliate against Lana for even existing. Plus, the thought of Lana in Evan's arms was infuriating, humiliating. Her feelings were being ridden like a roller coaster ride and she hated it.

Fumbling for something to say, she yelled, "For cryin' out loud, Evan! That there girl is buck naked!" It wasn't what she had intended; but at least it had slightly decreased the pressure that was building in the back of her head.

"Then grab something to cover her with!" he snapped back. "I certainly can't give up the blanket! Besides, I need something to press against the bullet wounds."

Diana hurriedly looked around, her mind racing through the variety of nothingness in the woods to choose from. Then, hurrying over to where Ches lay, she grabbed several handfuls of sticky webbing and a piece of his tattered shirt. Then, she ran back to Evan and Lana. Angrily, she tossed the piece of torn cloth at him, then she picked the sticky substance from her hands and randomly placed it on Lana's breasts and private area.

Evan irritably shook his head. "Now, she looks like she belongs on some type of stupid commercial. Come on, we don't have time for this. Grab the guns and find the car keys. Trey probably has them in his pocket."

Diana knelt at Trey's side and quickly searched through his pants pockets and found the keys. His eyes slightly fluttered and he groaned: She was glad to see the color was slightly returning to his skin.

"It'll be okay, darlin'." She brushed a lock of hair from his face. "Just hang on." Then, she grabbed Trey's gun and hers and hurriedly followed Evan to the car.

"You stay with Lana while I go get the other two. And, stay alert. Spence and the others could be returning at any time."

Evan then disappeared back into the trees. Moments passed; and, quickly returning with Trey, he gently placed him in the back seat of the car. Then, he ran back for Ches's body.

"Eww, that there fella's lookin' gross," Diana pointed out from the passenger's seat when Evan returned. "Does he have'ta ride with us? Ya'll can't put him in the trunk or somethin'?"

Evan slightly grinned. "That might be a good idea. Pop the trunk."

Diana hopped from the car, hurried to the back and opened the trunk lid. "There's all kindsa' junk in here."

"Well then, shove it to the side or toss it. And, what

about Sarge?"

"Oh, I let him loose," Diana answered. "That boy's at home here; he'll find his way back to the barn." Diana briefly stared at the fishing equipment, then hurriedly began to toss it out onto the road. "I'll send Marcus out here to pick all this stuff up. Daddy'd be mighty upset about the litter."

"Well, just get that stuff outta' the way so I can get him in there."

Evan's patience was running thin; tufts of the webbing were sticking to him everywhere and he feared Spence would show up. Plus, Ches stank.

Diana quickly made room and Evan placed Ches's body in the trunk, then he swiftly shut the lid.

The black Charger raced along the dirt road leading back toward the cabins. Evan remained silent as he concentrated on the road while also trying to avoid the numerous hardened glares from Diana. He didn't have to be able to read minds to imagine what she was thinking as a thousand questions probably galloped about inside her blonde head. However, he couldn't believe that she was able to remain quiet and not bombard him with at least one of them: he envisioned her cornering him later and driving him crazy with an overwhelming list.

Trey leaned against the rear passenger door, his eyes closed against the beads of sweat streaming his face. He lowly moaned as his body fought the painful recovery that was beginning, while Lana remained quiet.

Evan glanced in the rearview mirror, checking to see if she was okay. Her gunshot wounds were severe; and, if she were a normal human, they would have needed immediate medical attention. Though, since she was part arachnid, the wounds would most likely heal. That was one good thing about being a black widow.

Evan wanted to scold Diana for shooting her; however, she did what any normal human being would have done, and for that, he certainly couldn't say anything.

The cabins were now just half a mile away and Diana had held her tongue as long as humanly possible. A flood of questions pressed against the dam inside her, ready to break at any moment. She tapped the heel of her riding boot against the floor and her hands fidgeted nervously with the hem of her jacket. Then suddenly, the mental gates, suppressing the waterway of words broke, and a flood of questions spilled into the silence.

"So, is the guy in the trunk really dead, or what?" she asked.

Evan just looked at her, surprised by her candor.

"Well?" she pressed. "I asked ya'll if he's dead."

Evan thought about that briefly, wanting to answer her without invoking the onslaught of too many questions.

"Well...yes...and no," he quickly added. "Ches was bitten by a black widow spider; and, not just one, but two. And one was a black widow female, which is even more lethal." He glanced over at her, hoping he had satisfied her curiosity, however, most certain he hadn't.

Suddenly Lana interrupted their conversation. He was relieved.

"Evan?" they barely heard her say. She was carefully feeling the wounds to her head.

"I'm right here, Lana." His gaze briefly shot to the rearview mirror and he watched her.

"I'm sorry," she whispered.

He turned the car onto the dirt road leading toward the cabins which were just ahead.

"It's okay. Don't worry about it."

Her voice was broken, "Is Ches okay?"

Before he could answer, her eyes closed and she slipped into unconsciousness.

Chapter 7

Booger pulled Marty's Camaro to the side of the road and stared at the massive stain of quickly drying blood on the road.

"Damn…what…what…happened…?" he glanced over at Marty who was sitting in the passenger seat. He was leaning against the door and had his eyes closed.

"What is it?" Marty irritably opened his eyes and followed Booger's gaze to the blood on the road. Slowly and painfully, he leaned forward while holding his shoulder. Then, he added, "Looks like there was a massacre. I hope it was one of those smart-asses we had the other day.

Go check it out quick; then get me to the hospital."

Booger quickly opened his door and followed the trail of blood leading into the forest. Bursting into the clearing, he suddenly came to a halt.

The afternoon sun was beating down through a large gap in the trees; and, the smell of blood and rotting tissue was thick in the air. Enormous amounts of flies were collecting on Colette's huge form which was already beginning to decay.

"Oh…my…my…God!" Booger stuttered as he immediately placed his hand over his nose and mouth. "Ugh!" He rapidly spun on his heels and ran back to the car.

“Mar…ty!” he shouted. “You…have…ta…see… this!”

Marty opened one eye and glared at Booger who was running toward the car. Booger was shouting; however, *he* wasn’t rolling his window down, his shoulder was in too much pain.

“What the hell, Booger?”

In several strides, Booger reached the car and flung the door open; and spraying a shower of spittle over everything, including Marty, he shouted, “Mar… ty! You…have…ta…ta…see…this! It’s…it’s…one… of…the…sp…sp…spiders.”

Marty put his good arm up to protect himself from the spray of saliva. “Damn, Booger! Slow down! You’re given me a shower here.”

“But…but…you…have…ta…see! One…of…them… is…is…dead!”

Marty’s other eye opened; and groaning, he awkwardly climbed out.

“Did ya see if it’s a male or female?” he asked, as he followed behind.

Booger replied over his shoulder, No. I…didn’t… see…the…marking…on…its…stomach? All…I…saw… was…its…missing…head.”

“It’s missing head? Damn! That must’ve been a helluva fight!” Marty exclaimed. Regardless of his pain, he quickened his pace. “It had better not be Spence. That’s all I have’ta say.”

Suddenly, the trees to their left bowed and

cracked. Spence, still in his arachnid form, burst through the thick brush.

Marty and Booger stumbled backward to hide and watched as Spence quickly began to transform back into his human state.

"Marty, Booger," he called to them. "Get out here. I need ya ta get me some clothes…and what the hell were those gunshots I heard?"

"Ya…want…my…vest…Spence?" Booger quickly volunteered.

"Of course, Booger," Spence remarked.

Booger immediately removed his vest and handed it to Spence. Spence slipped it on. It was snug, unable to be closed in the front.

"And, give me your pants, Booger. You're closer ta my size than Marty."

Booger's mouth dropped open and he stammered, "But…but…Spence."

"What's the matter, Booger? As long as you're wearin' underwear, that's all that counts."

Booger briefly looked at Spence in the hopes he was kidding. With no sign of it being a joke, he slowly removed his jeans.

Spence snatched the pants from him and wrenched himself into them. They were tight and though he was able to get them zipped, he was unable to get them buttoned. His abrupt stare challenged any remark from either of them.

"Well, it's better'n bein' naked," Marty remarked.

Spence eyed him suspiciously, making sure there was no pun intended on his behalf. Then, he asked, "I asked what those gunshots were." He glanced around at the broken-down brush and the trail of blood that had been left behind by Ches. "And, where's Colette?"

Booger's gaze cut to Marty and their eyes briefly locked. Booger began to speak, but Marty, mustering the energy, raised his good hand as a sign for Booger to wait. Then, he spoke. "Well, we haven't seen Colette, Spence—not since we took off after the girl. And, we were going to see who was lying beyond the trees. Booger thought it might be Evan?"

Spence angrily scowled at them both. "No, it's not Evan! The slippery little bastard got away."

"Well…then…Sp…Spence," Booger stuttered, "who…who's…over…there?" He pointed toward the clearing where Colette's body lay.

"Whaddya mean, who's over there? One of those no good, pretty boys should be over there wrapped in one of my cocoons." Spence abruptly turned on his heels and headed in the direction that Booger was pointing."

"Uh…it…doesn't…look…like…one…one…of… them," Booger replied as he quickly fell in step behind Marty who was following closely behind Spence.

Spence marched along the path that was now snaking through the brush and forest. Anger stiffened his shoulder blades and his footsteps were widespread.

Bursting through the broken down brush, the three arrived in the clearing.

"Oh, my God," Marty whispered as his hand flew to cover his nose and mouth. The smell was atrocious. He could already tell by Spence's reaction who was lying before them; however, he couldn't help but ask, "Who is that?" He turned toward Spence, who immediately spun around to face him and Booger.

Spence's eyes were black as charcoal and his heated breath seethed through his clenched teeth. "Who did this?"

Marty and Booger back stepped and Marty quickly responded. "Booger found her. He was taking me to the hospital and we stopped when we saw all the blood. Booger found her like that and came to get me."

Spence's gaze shot back to the opened cocoon where Ches had been. "What happened to the guy who was in my cocoon?"

"He...wasn't...here...Sp...Spence," Booger's voice quaked with each stuttered word.

Spence remained quiet. Then, without turning, he spoke. His tone was marked. "Marty? Do ya have a gas can in your trunk?"

"Sure do, Spence," Marty answered.

"Is there any gas in it?"

"Should be."

"Then Booger, go and get it, pour it over her and light it," Spence ordered.

"But...but...Spence...

"Just do it! Then, I'll meet you two back at my place."

"But, I need ta go to the hospital, Spence," Marty said, "My shoulder hurts like hell."

Spence briefly stared at him, "Then hurry and get there. And, then, meet at my place after."

Spence swiftly removed the pants and vest he had on and tossed them at Booger; then, he rapidly transformed into the beast. And, releasing a horrifying screech, he disappeared into the forest.

"Hurry and get the gas can, Booger." Marty muffled from behind his hand. "The smell is terrible; and, it's really creepy around here."

Booger immediately ran to the car to retrieve the gas can then quickly returned. Then, dousing Colette's immense arachnid form in gasoline, he snatched the pack of matches in the air that Marty tossed him, struck one of the sticks, and watched her go up in flames.

Chapter 8

With Diana's help, Evan was able to get Trey, Ches and Lana settled into his small cabin. Lana was in his bedroom, Trey on the couch and Ches on the oval rug in the middle of the living room floor.

He and Diana had spoken very little during the time it had taken to get everyone inside. And, as long as he had known Diana, he knew she was stewing, like a pot of soup that was turned up too high and was ready to boil over.

At the first opportunity, Evan slipped into the bathroom, retrieved water, washcloth, bandages and medicine and hurried into his bedroom. Fortunately, he had repaired the door and was able to shut and lock it behind him. Then, switching on the light, he went to the bed and sat on the edge next to Lana.

She was lying on her side with her back to him. And, she was still unconscious. He attempted to examine the wounds to her head; however, the blood was caking in her hair and over the bullet holes. It made it very difficult to see the wounds.

Dipping the washcloth in the warm water, he gently washed away some of the blood. Then, carefully, separating the hair, he examined her wounds. He knew that she, like him, had the power to heal herself; however, he was completely surprised at how quickly she was mending. The bullet wounds were slowly closing and the blood had begun to clot.

"Lana?" He gently touched her shoulder.

She slowly rolled over and blinked her eyes trying to get them to focus.

"Evan?"

"I'm here," he answered. He fingered a few strands of her damp hair and removed them from her face.

Lana slipped her hand within his.

"I'm sorry about everything." Her voice was strained.

Evan didn't respond.

Then, she quietly asked, "Where is Ches? We have to help him." Her full, dark eyes were pleading.

Evan's first impulse was to pull away, avoid her gaze which could draw him in and make him vulnerable to her every whim. However, having her here now and safe, he wanted to drown within those deep dark pools, feast upon those irises of melting chocolate that caused his insides to rumble and his head to spin.

But, Ches's presence was making him irritable; and, the idea of him needing to draw upon Lana's blood was even more annoying.

"He's in the living room—he and Trey both," he stated bitterly. "Trey will need some time to heal; and, Ches will need some help." He then added, "That's if you're still determined to help him." Truthfully, he hoped she wasn't.

"But, for right now, you need to rest."

Evan stood. "I should go and let you sleep."

"No. I need to help him now." Lana attempted to sit up; however, she painfully grabbed at her head. "Ow."

"Just hold on." He gently pressed her back toward the pillow. "Your healing won't take long. Then, you can go help lover boy."

Ignoring his comment, Lana carefully laid her head back, and for a moment, closed her eyes. The situation was a mess. She knew Evan was still upset with her about Ches. And, she had attacked him and Diana and had almost killed them.

Several minutes passed as she clung to Evan's hand, making certain he didn't leave, and giving herself a moment to think of something to say. Then, taking a deep breath, she spoke in a whisper. "Evan, I'm sorry. I'm really sorry. I've never meant to hurt you. And, I certainly didn't mean to try and hurt you and Diana in the forest. I just couldn't stop myself. It was like something was making me do it." She remained silent for a moment then asked, "Will you ever forgive me?" Her hand gripped his tighter. "You probably hate me."

He thought about that for a moment, thought about her in Ches's arms. He had been hurt then; however, she was here now. And, regardless of her injuries, she was beautiful *and* he knew he loved her. Her face was only inches from his, and her breath was sweet upon his skin. More than anything, he wanted to kiss her, place his lips to hers and show her how much he cared. However, he wouldn't.

"I forgive you." He got up to leave. "Now, you need to get some rest."

Lana was stunned at his reply. It had been too quick, too callous. She knew this wasn't resolved. More than likely, things were still brewing inside him.

Holding firmly to his hand, like a lifeline for a drowning man, she sat up and whispered. "Evan, please. Please, don't go." She would attempt to use her powers of persuasion on him. Holding the blanket to cover her body, she pulled him back to the bed and slid against him.

Evan watched her eyes closely, wondering if she knew what she was doing. "Lana, please don't try to trick me."

Suddenly, she blinked her eyes and moved away from him. She had embarrassed herself. "I'm sorry." She lowered her head and spoke to her hands. "I thought it would be the only way I could get you to stay with me."

Evan gently turned her face towards him and looked into her eyes. His voice was soft and soothing. "You don't have to try and trick me to make me stay with you."

She turned her head. "But, you've left me before, and didn't come back."

He looked at her mildly confused.

"Are you referring to when I left Ches's?" He didn't wait for a response. "I left because you and Ches were in the bedroom together."

"I know," she replied, "but, it wasn't what you think. Ches was just consoling me."

"Half dressed?" he quickly retorted. His extremely handsome features darkened at the thought. "You were half dressed, also. So, what was I supposed to think?" His blood was beginning to heat as he was becoming more irate. "Maybe this *is* a mistake."

"It wasn't like that..." Lana started.

A sharp knock sounded upon the door.

"Evan?" Diana's voice snapped. "Evan, are ya'll in there?"

"What's the matter?"

"Whaddya'll mean, what's the matter? Ya'll left me out here alone with a dead guy. And, the other one's spittin up all over ya'lls couch and moanin like a bull in heat. What in the world ya'll mean, what's the matter?"

She banged on the door again.

Lana secured the quilt around her and attempted to slide from the bed. Taking three awkward steps, she was spinning and careening forward. Evan moved quickly and caught her before she hit the floor.

"Whoa! Hang on just a minute." He set her back on the bed. "I told you, you still need some time to heal. I'll go check on them. You just stay here and get better." He left the room and closed the door behind him.

Lana's eyes were closed in an attempt to stop the

room from spinning. Her words trailed behind him in barely a whisper.

"Evan, what does that mean? 'It was a mistake.'"

Diana glowered at her. Her cobalt eyes were sharp shards of ice. "What was a mistake?" she spat.

"Nothing," Lana answered lowly, her eyes still closed.

Diana walked to the side of the bed and glared down at her. "Have ya'll been kissin' my Evan?"

Lana opened her eyes and just looked at her.

"Well, ya'll creep me out, Lana." Her tone was acidic. "Too bad ya'll didn't die."

"Ahh man!" Evan groaned at the sight of the mess on his couch and floor. Hurrying into the bathroom, he returned with a small plastic trash can and a roll of paper towels.

"If ya gotta throw up, throw up in this!" He set the trash can down on the floor next to Trey then busied himself with cleaning up the mess on the floor.

Trey quickly leaned over and vomited; then, he laid his head back and stared blindly up at the ceiling. "Oh my God; I feel like shit." Immediately reaching for the trash can, he vomited again.

Diana appeared from within the bathroom with two washcloths and immediately went to his side.

"Here, sweetie." She laid a cool cloth across his forehead and dabbed his mouth and cheeks with the other. Then, she went to the kitchen, opened the freezer door, and retrieved some ice. Placing the cubes in a glass from the cupboard, she took them to him.

"Here, suck on these. It might help."

"Thank you," he croaked as he gazed up at her. His eye-color had returned to normal; however, his face was the color of milk. "You've helped me so much. You're an angel." A slight smile briefly touched his lips until his stomach pitched again and he vomited once more.

"Oh, geez," he moaned. "There can't be anything else in my gut. What is going on?"

"It's the venom," Evan remarked, as he opened the front door for some fresh air. The living room was beginning to smell. "You'll be sick for quite a few days, especially with as much venom, I assume it was Colette, injected into you. Most people couldn't handle as much as you did. You can see what she and Spence did to Ches." He motioned in Ches's direction. "We'll be lucky if Lana can help him.

"Oh, and, Trey, I wanted to ask you: Do you know what happened to Spence?"

"I don't know, man. I didn't see him." Trey took a breath and swallowed the nausea rising in the back of his throat. He wasn't around when I got there."

"Yeah, I know. He was chasing after us for a while," Evan replied.

Lana suddenly appeared at the bedroom door.

“Evan?” She was wrapped in the quilt from his bed.

Quickly, he went to her side and slipped his arm around her waist to support her.

“You should still be in bed.”

“No. I’m fine. I need to help.”

“If you insist,” he replied.

All eyes turned his way. Ignoring their stares, he assisted Lana to where Ches lay on the floor. Pulling the blanket securely around her, she knelt down beside him.

Briefly, Lana stared into Ches’s face. His features were drawn, near skeletal, the color of ash. And, his eyes, which were normally warm and sparked with life, rested within deep-set dark sockets which were sunken and closed.

A large lump formed in her throat and she fought the tears that begged to be released. Gently, pushing aside a lock of blonde hair from his forehead, she placed a kiss just beneath where her fingers were. “I’m sorry, Ches,” she whispered into his ear. “I’ll do everything I can to help you.” Then, she turned to look at Evan.

“I can’t transform in here,” she stated. “Should we go outside?”

Evan’s eyes were black and his body rigid as he stood with his arms crossed while leaning against the bathroom door.

“Yeah,” he replied curtly. “Let’s get this over with.”

“What’s happening with Ches?” Trey pushed

himself to an elbow.

Diana was on the edge of the couch beside him.

"Don't ya'll worry, honey. They're gonna' try and bring him back, fix him."

Trey began to shiver and droplets of sweat were forming upon his upper lip.

Diana placed her hand to his forehead then stated, "Ya'll are burnin' up. I'll get ya a blanket."

"Evan." Her tone was sardonic. "Trey needs a blanket. Is it okay if I git one from your armoire?"

"Its fine," came as a low growl.

Diana's attitude was adding fuel to his fire, causing his already simmering blood to nearly boil. His thoughts were centered on Lana having to transform. It would endanger her—bring her to the level of an insect, a beast. Then, she would have to draw the venom from Ches's system and replace it with her own blood, causing her and Ches's bond to be inseparable.

This would cause Ches's desire to escalate, heighten to insurmountable levels. He would want Lana more than anything, especially as an arachnid male. The longing for her as a female would be nearly impossible to control, causing him to act irrationally, or possibly deadly.

Evan had been a black widow for a little over a century, and yet at times it was difficult for *him* to control the beast within himself. So, it would be extremely difficult for Ches. This attraction would be different, stronger, a blood bond between beasts.

Evan shook his head, attempting to clear his mind and emotions and concentrate on what was best for all those involved.

"Are you sure you wanna' do this?" Moving to Lana's side he crouched down beside her. "Lana, you know this will change him forever; and, he will never go back. He may even become dangerous and try to hurt you."

Lana looked into his chestnut-colored eyes that normally danced with an array of color; however, now they were cool, unreadable. She knew he didn't like this, knew the whole situation was eating at him like a termite eats at wood. However, she knew she had to help Ches no matter what.

Nodding her head, she whispered, "Yes. It's my fault this happened to him and I need to fix it somehow." She paused then quietly asked, "Will you please help me?"

Without answering, Evan rose to his feet. Then, he bent and hoisted Ches over his shoulder. They were nearly the same size; and, if it hadn't been for his arachnid strength, it would have been nearly impossible for him to get Ches outside without dragging him.

To Evan, the idea sounded kind of nice.

Chapter 9

"No. I'm not leaving you alone with him," Evan angrily shook his head at Lana who was attempting to stare him in the eyes—use her power of persuasion on him. "He's liable to hurt you; or, you're liable to hurt yourself."

Lana gently held to his arm and pulled him toward her.

A low snarl ripped from Diana's throat as she stood with Trey at the front door watching.

"I agree, Lana," Trey wearily remarked as he used the front door frame and Diana for support. "You should listen to him."

"No, Trey," she replied softly as she continued to try and catch Evan's stare. Ches was still slung over his shoulder, making it difficult for him move quick enough to twist away from her. "I tried to kill him last time and I can't let that happen again."

Trey glanced at Diana in mild confusion as he jerked a thumb in Lana's direction. "*She* can kill *him*?"

Without responding, Diana only nodded her head.

"Lana..." Evan's tone was a warning. "I'll toss him, if you don't knock it off."

Bingo! Lana suddenly had him as her eyes locked with his and he immediately swore beneath his breath.

The strength in Evan's body depleted as he slipped to a knee and Ches rolled from his arms to the ground.

Lana placed her arms around his neck and locked her fingers beneath his hair. Her face was within inches from his and her sweet breath was warm upon his face. "Evan, you have to listen to me. I'll be fine. Now, go inside."

Evan's head swam; and, while his human strength was like mush, his inner beast raged to be released. A war was waging inside him.

Suddenly, he was powerless to the soft words she spoke and the controlling supremacy in her eyes. It was like listening to someone speak through a long hollow tube, a distorted echo.

"Evan," she spoke in barely a whisper. "Please allow me to do this alone. Diana will need you to help her with Trey. And, I don't want you getting hurt. Please." Her eyes were still locked with his as she removed a hand from behind his neck and placed it to his cheek. Then, she motioned with her other hand for Diana to come out into the yard.

"You only have a few seconds to get him inside. As soon as I look away, he'll begin to function normally. So, you'll have to hurry."

"How do ya'll know what'll happen?" Diana retorted.

"Because," Lana replied, "I've done this to him before; so, we only have a minute or two. Then, *you* have to keep him inside."

Diana's brows creased. "*Me?* Why should I do anything ya'll ask?"

Lana's eyes became as narrowed slits; and losing her patience, she angrily snapped her head in Diana's direction. "Because, you love him too. That's why. Now, take him inside."

A round moment passed as a staring match ensued.

"Diana…" Trey called to her. "…Come on; just do what she asks." Coughing, he vomited off the side of the porch. "Oh, shit. Let's just get this over with." He wiped his mouth with the back of his hand. "Come on; just get him inside so she can help Ches."

Immediately spinning, Diana grabbed Evan by the arm and helped him to his feet. He wobbled unsteadily as if he were balancing on tinker toys.

"Don't ya'll think ya've gotten away with anything, Lana," Diana remarked over her shoulder. "I'm only doin' this for Evan."

Lana watched them go into the cabin and close the door behind them. She then turned and briefly glanced into the nearby forest, listening to the wildlife busy with its daily tasks and making sure there was no present danger. Then, taking a deep breath, she slipped the blanket from her body and concentrated on her inner creature.

Immediately, she began to transform.

The transformation came quickly as the webbing poured from the hour-glass tattoo upon her stomach and wrapped itself around her body. It completely consumed her, snaking from her torso down along her thighs, calves and feet, then upward along her breasts, neck and face. Her breathing was measured and deep and her eyes, flashing from black to crimson, sparked with animation till they were completely covered.

A brief moment passed and suddenly she burst from within her cocoon, careened through the air and thudded to the ground. She was big and black, majestic—an enormous black widow spider. The forest around her immediately succumbed to silence.

Lana's eight eyes darted to and fro as her eyes scanned the area and came to rest on Ches. Then, releasing an ear-piercing screech, she moved in his direction.

Within seconds, he was swiftly encased within her cocoon; and, the two billion tiny teeth, lining the inside of her mouth, clicked together in a sickening display of hunger.

Lana's fangs, quickly emerging from within her mouth, throbbed with energy and poison. They glinted against the darkness of her exoskeleton, aching for blood and nourishment while she needed to satisfy her overwhelming appetite.

Loud screeching raged outside the cabin; and, having fully recovered from what he considered to be *Lana's curse*, Evan stepped toward the front door. Diana was suddenly there, placing herself between him and the only exit. Evan attempted to push past her.

“Let me by, Diana,” his tone was marked. “I don’t wanna have to force you out of the way.”

“Fine! Go to ya’lls girlfriend! See if I care if she chews ya’ll up like chewin’ tobacca and spits ya out!” Spinning on her heels, she marched into the kitchen.

Trey wearily observed the confrontation from the couch.

“Hey…” His throat was scratchy. “…Are you two like, ex-boyfriend and girlfriend? Because, if not, you two sure act like it.”

“No!” Diana slammed the cupboard door, where she had grabbed a glass for a drink of water. Her southern drawl escalated. “Who in their right mind would wanna’ be with someone who turns into an ugly lookin’ spider?”

Trey winced, “Ouch. That hadda’ hurt.”

Evan cringed at Diana’s words; however, a confrontation with her at the moment was unimportant, trivial to what might be going on outside. Opening the front door, he stepped out onto the small porch; and though he himself was a black widow and had many times given in to the animalistic tendencies of the beast, he slightly recoiled at what he saw. Racing down the steps, he ran across the yard. “Lana! Stop!”

Quickly, Lana turned and her eight eyes rapidly assessed the situation and him. And, positioning Ches beneath her massive chest, she guarded him like a mother with her child, or possibly like a snack you tuck in your pocket for later.

Evan spoke to her softly, attempting to coax her into releasing Ches and concentrating on the task at hand. "I don't wanna' take him from you, Lana. You need to help him, get him breathing." Releasing a loud screech, she backed away and reared. Her fangs were bared and her eyes blazed. Evan searched his mind for anything that would keep her from bolting, tearing through the forest, or ripping Ches to shreds. Slowly, he stepped toward her. "Lana, think of your brother. Think of Samuel."

Lana wearily observed Evan through a thick cloud, while her mind and emotions struggled against the beast's will of wanting to run and take its prey and also ravage Evan and consume his blood.

She watched as he moved closer. His hands were outstretched toward her as he gently spoke her name. The beast within her wanted to charge, wanted to spin its webbing and wrap him in her cocoon, while the desire to feast upon him was riveting, nearly impossible to control.

"Evan, why are you out here?" Her thoughts raged against the insurmountable urge to strike. "I told you to stay inside."

Then, Evan had spoke Samuel's name.

"Samuel?" The sound of her brother's name suddenly made her pause, nearly caused her to weep, for if she couldn't control the animalistic instincts, she would never be able to find Samuel.

"Evan, help me," she whispered. Speaking was

like being inside a tunnel, the plastic tubes on a playground. However, she knew Evan could understand her—hear her through his inner beast.

"Lana," Evan warily called, "Ches needs your help and so does Samuel."

Lana backed away as the eight marble-like eyes in her head frantically scanned the area for a means of escape, and the urge to run was over-whelming. The creature within her shrieked in anger, attempted to battle against the human will invading its inner strength.

"No!" the scream tore from her throat, as she fought the beast. "No! I won't let you control me!"

Evan stepped closer; his words were soothing. "I'm here, Lana. What can I do?" Lana's struggle with her inner self was difficult, something he was all too familiar with.

Lana knew that only she could do what needed to be done. She concentrated on being firm, unyielding, and stood erect with resolve in her mind. No longer would the black widow rule her, she would rule it.

Slowly placing Ches on the ground before her, she forced the massive arachnid creature to step back.

Evan watched her closely, realizing she now had control. Slowly, he moved toward Ches's body.

"Lana, it's time for you to remove the poison from Ches. You need to bite him without injecting any poison into him. Bite through the cocoon."

Lana reared and shook her head. Then, slowly

moving toward the wrapped corpse, she threw her head back and, without warning, drove her fangs deep into her prey.

Her enormous body quaked against the urge that nearly drove her to inject him with her poison, ingest of his bodily fluids and drain him dry. However, she fought against the uncontrollable urge and diligently began to suck the venom from his system, one drink at a time.

To partake of another black widow's venom was vile, revolting to her taste buds. However, the few remaining droplets of Ches's blood that intermingled with the poison, tasted good. It took every effort for her to replace it with her own.

Suddenly, Ches awoke to darkness, pain.

"Oh, God! What's happening to me?" The words screamed from his quavering lips and his body shook. He tried to recall anything that would, for a brief moment, help to alleviate the pain, the pain that was causing him to cry out and wish for immediate death. However, his thoughts were like scrambled eggs and the effort to live was becoming too difficult.

He could feel the large set of fangs that were sunk within his side; they were thick as harpoons and sharp as spears. They pulsed and plunged deeper within his side, while extracting the venom from his system, then replacing it with new blood.

He could hear a voice yell, *Stop!* And, the fangs suddenly ripped from his body. Then, plummeting downward, he hit the ground and remained still.

"Help me," he whispered to the darkness. "Somebody, help me…"

Chapter 10

"Oh, shut up!" Spence hollered at his two dogs as his bare feet pounded against the few steps leading up to the trailer. Angrily, he pushed through the front door and headed directly for the bathroom.

Switching the water on in the shower, he stepped in and yanked the curtain closed behind him.

The water careened over his large body; and, grabbing the washcloth and soap, he irritably worked to scrub the blood from his skin.

"Damn it!" he shouted, as the water ran over his hair and face and spurted from his lips. He banged his fists against the fiberglass wall and the enclosure shook. "Damn you, Colette! Why did you have to go and get yourself killed?"

Palming some shampoo through his wet hair, he rinsed it, then shut the water off. And, stepping from the shower, he grabbed a towel, wrapped it around himself and walked out into the living room.

Water dripped from his body and lay in puddles along where his feet had stepped; however, he didn't care. His thoughts were absorbed with other things—such as revenge.

Various items of Colette's: cigarettes, lighter, a bright pink sweater, and a few other items were scattered about the living room. Spence looked at them with disgust. Quickly gathering them up, he carried them to the kitchen. There, he pressed the metal level to the garbage can, watched as the lid banged open, and dumped the items inside. Then, removing the garbage liner, he tied it closed, walked to the front door and dropped it off the side of the porch.

Spence slammed the front door. Then, he snatched the phone from the coffee table and plopped down into the recliner. His fingers hurriedly punched at several numbers on the receiver and his father answered after a few rings.

"Hello?"

"Hey Pop," Spence replied.

"What's up, Spence?"

"Some shit's gone down, Pop, and Colette's dead."

There was silence on the other end for a brief moment, then his father responded.

"That's too bad, Spence. But, no sense cryin' over spilled milk."

"Yeah, well somethin's happened and I need ya to come over. Bring Eddie and Travis with ya; I'm gonna need their help."

"Now, Spence, ya know I'm still on probation, so I need ta lay low for awhile."

"Yeah, I know. I just want ya ta come out here and check somethin' out. Eddie and Travis can help me out with what I need to do. Can ya make it around two?"

"Sure, son. I'll see ya then."

Spence hit the off button on the phone; then, he

laid his head back and closed his eyes. Images of his battling Evan swirled in his mind like a carousel at an amusement park; and, despite the few irksome feelings he had toward Colette being gone, he grinned.

Ches burst from within Lana's cocoon and landed a few feet from where Lana stood in her arachnid form. He was gigantic, larger than Lana or Evan, and he stood tall, regal and stately. His exoskeleton was black as night and shiny; and, his eight eyes, darting between the two, were unlike Evan's and Lana's crimson-red ones. They were copper-colored, reddish-gold gems that shifted slightly in an attempt to focus; then, they quickly centered in on Evan.

For a black widow spider, Ches was beautiful.

Evan remained on guard, watching for any sign Ches would lunge. He shouted to Lana. "Lana! Get back! He might attack."

Ches's head snapped in Evan's direction as his eight eyes rolled within their sockets attempting to settle on Evan as he moved. A loud, grandiose cry tore from his throat and the two billion teeth within Ches's mouth began to rapidly click as his fangs, dripping with venom, appeared.

"Now, Ches..." Evan slowly took a few steps backward; his arms were outstretched. "Don't make me do anything I might regret."

Evan glanced at Lana who was quickly beginning

to transform back into her human state. The intake of venom and loss of blood causing her body to metamorphose was making her weak. Evan moved cautiously toward the blanket she had covered herself with, and slowly picking it up from the ground, he carefully stepped in her direction and wrapped it around her.

"Lana, we need to get you inside. Just don't make any sudden moves." He slipped his arm around her waist and gradually helped her toward the cabin.

Ches's eyes shone brightly in the evening's light and he curiously watched as Evan assisted Lana toward the cabin. Then, releasing a melodious, almost sweet sounding call, he slowly stepped in their direction.

Diana had appeared at the front door and was watching. "Holy cow patties!" Her voice was a harsh whisper, "That there is Ches?"

"Yes," Evan responded lowly. "Now, we have'ta get Lana inside. But, don't move too quickly."

Diana's faced soured and she wanted to protest as he handed Lana off to her like a baton in a relay race. However, she didn't. Immediately, she closed the door behind them.

Evan then, quickly, spun on his heels to face Ches who had moved closer to where he stood.

"Ches," Evan's voice was low, calming. "Think about who you are—what you are—a human. You have to revert back to your human form." It was like speaking to a child, a child who was teetering on a ledge.

Ches observed Evan through a gray haze. "What's happened to me?" His head spun as a thousand questions raced through his mind and he attempted to concentrate on each and every one—an effort to retain any human traits he still possessed. He tried desperately to keep his eyes in focus; however, it was extremely difficult.

An unfamiliar call, yet comprehensible to his ears, tore from his throat. It was a cry for help, a plea for Evan or anyone to release him from this bondage of being trapped within this hideous figure from hell. He forced his attention to remain on Evan, while the wildlife, that had been deadly quiet, all of a sudden perked to life, shrieking and chattering like the crazies at an out-of-control bachelor party. What was Evan trying to say or do?

Ches used every ounce of energy to utilize the human strength within him, to battle the characteristics of the beast aiming to control his body.

"Ughh!" he groaned as his eight legs suddenly buckled beneath him and he toppled to the ground. For a brief moment he laid there; then, his body began its metamorphosis back to human form. It came slowly until he lay in the grass panting.

"Oh God, what happened?" he finally spoke.

Evan walked over and looked down at him lying in the grass. "Welcome to my world—you've now become a black widow spider."

Ches's eyes narrowed as he glanced up at Evan standing over him. His voice was hoarse. "And, I guess you're to blame for this?"

"Nope," Evan replied. "It was all Lana. She wanted you alive. So you'll have'ta speak to her about it."

"Hm," Ches stared past Evan toward the graying sky.

"So, what does this mean for me?"

"Welp, I guess it means a lifetime of being a freak." Evan's brief smile was sardonic. Then, his face washed of all expression.

"Now, for the downside: You can't let anyone know what you've become. You've become an outcast. Secondly, the fear that someday you won't be able to return to your human self is something that'll haunt your dreams every night. You'll lie in your bed stirring, terrified to be awakened to something other than what you went to bed as..."

Evan paused and thought for a moment. "Oh, and every time you transform, it hurts like hell, the ripping and tearing of flesh and bone is excruciatingly painful, until you learn to adjust to it—give in and let it take over. And then, to top it all off, what you become is hideous and repulsive, an appalling looking beast.

Evan walked over and grabbed the shorts hanging on the peg just outside the front door of the cabin. Then, he walked back to Ches and dropped them on the ground at his feet.

"So, there you have it—compliments of the United States Military."

Ches quickly pulled the shorts on and attempted to sit up; however, his head spun like the numbers on a roulette table and he laid back down.

"Oh, man. I don't feel so hot. I think I have a fever."

Reaching out on impulse to touch Ches's forehead, Evan then thought better of it and withdrew his hand.

Noticing his reaction, Ches remarked, "That's okay, amigo. I'm a big boy. I don't need your doctoring."

Evan scoffed.

Suddenly, Lana burst from inside the cabin and ran down the steps. Her face was white with worry as she hurried toward where Ches and Evan were.

"Is he okay?" She gently touched Evan's arm as she quickly slipped past him. Then, dropping to her knees, she wrapped her arms around Ches's neck and pulled him toward her. "Are you okay? I was so worried."

"Yeah," he replied weakly. "I'll survive."

She placed her hand on his forehead. "Oh my gosh, you're burning up." Her eyes were anxious as she turned toward Evan and asked, "Is he going to be okay?"

"He'll be fine." Evan's eyes briefly sparked and for a moment his irises turned black.

"Then, will you help me get him inside?" she asked.

Evan scowled. "Inside where?"

Lana's gaze narrowed. "Inside the cabin."

She wondered if he was trying to start a fight or was he just being his old cynical self? Regardless, she wasn't giving in.

Evan wanted to say *no*, but somehow he couldn't. He was a slave to her now, willing to give her anything she wanted or needed; however, his feelings were in a quandary and he didn't like it.

Without saying a word, he bent and took Ches's arm in his and assisted him to his feet. Ches groaned.

Lana scurried to standing; and, before taking Ches's other arm, she lightly touched Evan again. "Thank you."

"It's okay," he replied without looking at her. "We certainly can't let him go running around the countryside transforming and bringing the authorities down on us."

Lana nodded her head as she quietly pondered this, thinking of the ramifications.

Trey met them at the door. His strength still hadn't returned.

"Is he going to be okay?" he asked.

Evan grudgingly shrugged. "Should be."

"Thank God," Trey remarked.

"Where do ya'll wanna put him?" Diana asked as she popped her head out the door again. "How 'bout ya'lls bed, Evan?" Her eyes matched the mischief in her voice.

"No," Evan snapped.

A wicked grin crested her full lips. "Well then, where, Evan darlin'…"

"He can stay on the floor," he immediately retorted.

They all turned their heads to look at him and he returned their gaze with an irate glance.

"Well then, I have a little ol' suggestion," Diana volunteered. "How 'bout Trey honey stays over with me, and that way Ches here can have ya'lls couch?"

Evan glared at her through narrowed slits; her presence was working on his every nerve. "Fine," he answered. "He can stay on the couch until we figure something out."

"Thank you, amigo," Ches remarked.

Evan's near congeniality had finally fizzled to near nothingness and he stiffened. "And, ya better quit callin' me amigo…I'm not your friend."

"Well then, I beg your pardon," Ches replied, "please accept my apologies."

"Whatever." Evan gripped Ches's arm tighter and tugged him toward the door of the cabin and the living room. "This is only temporary."

"Understood," Ches answered.

Lana was watching them;, her guilt-ridden stare bore holes through Evan's skin.

Concentrating on getting Ches inside and onto the couch, Evan made it a point to avoid her hawking gaze.

"I have one question for you, Ches: Do you know where Spence might be?" Evan then asked.

"No. I couldn't tell ya', maybe his place..." Ches took a breath as he closed his eyes and laid his head back.

Evan remained quiet as he went into the kitchen.

Lana sat next to Ches as he lay on the couch. Occasionally, she brushed a strand of corn silk hair from his dampened forehead. His fever had escalated to nearly 106 degrees and for four days and four nights he fought against the arachnid beast that was consuming his body.

His fever finally had broken on the fifth day. It had been slightly afternoon while Evan was in town purchasing supplies, leaving her and Ches alone the entire day.

Nighttime was beginning to settle outside and Evan still hadn't returned. Lana glanced at the clock on the kitchen wall wondering where he might be.

"Lana," Ches's voice cracked. "Thank you for staying with me. You didn't have to do that."

"I just feel so bad about what's happened. Can you forgive me?" She faintly smiled.

"There's nothing to forgive." He gently touched her cheek. "I'm only concerned about you."

The silence was awkward as they each wondered what should be said next. Then, he spoke. "I really think I need a shower. Do you think it would be okay with Evan?"

"Yeah, sure," she responded. Quickly, she stood and watched as he slowly slid his feet to the floor and attempted to steady himself as he stood. Her hand reached for his as he wobbled slightly. Finally, he was able to stand erect.

"Gee. I feel like I just got off the merry-go-round."

He quietly laughed.

"Evan left some clothes for you on the vanity in the bathroom. He said they would have to do until you went home."

He quietly laughed again. "I can imagine he can't wait until then."

Lana fidgeted uneasily; for the entire time Ches was sick on the couch, Evan had been somewhat more irate than usual. She knew that it was partially from his sleeping sitting up in the recliner while she had taken his bed. However, she was aware that there was a deeper issue, something drilling at him like a tick—Ches.

Each morning would consist of a fifteen minute grumble session as he would achingly stretch then make his way to the bathroom. This was after he gave Ches a flicker of black iris voodoo. A look meant to inflict the uncontrollable anger he felt, and the pain of his stiff joints.

"Yeah," she finally responded. "I'm really sorry about that."

"No need to apologize. You never need to apologize to me, Lana." Smiling, he slipped into the bathroom and closed the door quietly behind him.

As soon as Ches disappeared into the bathroom, Lana slid from the hardback kitchen chair onto the couch and closed her eyes. She was dressed in the oversized white t-shirt Evan had given her to sleep in and she was extremely tired. Taking care of Ches for the past four days had been difficult, something she only knew how to do from the times she or her brother had been sick while their mother took care of them.

"Oh, Mom," she quietly whispered, "I miss you and Dad. And, I promise, no matter what, I'll find Samuel and take care of him." Brushing her arm across her eyes, she blinked back the tears that fought to come. "No. I won't cry. Crying won't find Samuel," she spoke to the ceiling as she laid her head back and closed her eyes.

Twenty minutes passed and Ches emerged from the bathroom. Steam rolled out from behind him as he appeared dressed in only the jeans that Evan had left for him. They fit quite well, snuggly against his muscular figure while the deep red male arachnid streaks accentuated his fantastic form

The perfect shading of his skin had returned, along with the sparkle in his azure-colored eyes. His hair was wet and slicked back and several wavy strands bounced lightly around his face. He looked incredible, "yumma'licious" as her friends from school would always say. He was gorgeous.

Briefly, she thought of her friends, wondering what would happen when school started and she wasn't there. This was to be their final year, her senior year; and she had wanted to graduate more than anything. Now it seemed trivial, almost like a lost, faraway dream.

She had thought about calling her best friend, Mia, tell her about her parents. Mia would be crushed;

she had known Lana's family since fifth grade when she and Lana had first become friends. However, she didn't want to put her in danger, danger from her, Evan, or Ches, and especially Spence. Maybe she'd consider calling her in a few days; right now Ches was standing before her studying her every move.

Lana had to catch her breath as she looked at him and his flawless smile lit the room. She watched somewhat mesmerized as he slipped his arms through the shirt he was carrying and pulled it on. Then, shaking his head to disband the variegated strands of hair that had fallen around his face, he smiled again.

Lana sat motionless as his bare feet patted lightly upon the wooden floor and he made his way to the couch to sit down beside her.

Gently, he took her hand and held it in his. His skin was warm to the touch, fresh from the water that had moments earlier caressed it. The musky scent of lavender lightly misted the air, reminding Lana of the flowers her mother grew in the backyard beneath their kitchen window, the ones she loved to smell as she came down for breakfast on summer mornings.

Silence filled the gap between them and Lana fidgeted with the fabric of the over-sized t-shirt she wore. Her mind raced to the last time they had been alone in the jeep. She had nearly been sitting in his lap. Then, when he left her, he had gently kissed her lips. It was brief, sweet, something she would remember and cherish always; though, she would never allow it to happen again. She needed to try and repress any feelings she felt toward him, attempt to make him understand that she cared for him and maybe even loved him; however, she loved Evan more.

Ches turned toward her and lightly placed his other hand on her cheek; then, he ran his hand through a few strands of her hair resting along her shoulder.

"Lana, please don't make me go home alone."

His azure blue eyes were shaded with unhappiness, dejection. She hated seeing it there, never wanted to be the cause of it. However, she knew she was. Quickly, she averted her gaze and stared at the clock unsure of how her power of persuasion would affect him. Maybe she could persuade him into being happy without her. She also wondered where Evan was.

"Lana, why won't you look at me?"

Her cheeks grazed pink as her eyes slowly turned and rested on his chest.

"I don't know what will happen. And," her voice became no more than a whisper, "I don't know what to say, how to respond."

Ches took her chin in his hand and tenderly lifted it upward until her eyes met his. "What do you mean?"

She slightly averted her gaze. "Well, I'm a black widow female, I kind of have a power that may influence you into doing things you may not want to do. Evan gets mad at me when I use it. Plus…," she paused, "…I love him, Ches…I just do."

He chuckled softly. "Well, regardless of how Evan

feels, why don't you let me be the judge of your so-called powers? I can almost assure you, I won't get angry. Plus," he looked into her eyes. "I know you love Evan and I'm certain he loves you. However..." He pulled her closer and pressed his cheek to hers, then his lips slipped within her hair and lightly touched her ear. His breath was warm. "I love you too, and I won't give up. I'll wait for you forever."

The pounding of Ches's heart rang within Lana's ears; and, the warmth of his freshened skin and dampened hair heightened her arachnid awareness.

"Ches...

Suddenly, Lana jumped as the front door opened and Evan stepped inside.

Chapter 11

The first thing Lana noticed when Evan came through the door was the severe case of black iris voodoo he shot Ches. She then, through her arachnid senses, noticed the rise in temperature of his blood and the increased rhythm of his heart. Slipping away from Ches, she quickly stood to her feet and fumbled out a greeting, "Hey, Evan. You were gone so long." Her face flushed crimson as she instantly made space between herself and the couch.

Without answering, Evan looked past her to Ches and remarked, "You're looking better."

"I'm feeling much better; thank you." Ches's eyes remained locked with his. "I was just asking Lana here if she would come home with me. And, she was just getting ready to answer before you walked in."

Evan's gaze cut to Lana though his question was directed toward Ches. "And, what did she say?"

"Well, like I said, she hasn't answered me yet; and, I would never think of pressuring her in any way. So, Lana, my dear..." He reached up for her hand and his lips lingered there briefly as he softly kissed it; then, he gently released it to her side. "...I will await an answer until you are ready." His smile was warm, comforting, however, not quite enough to settle the butterflies that were waging an all out flapping match within her stomach, or enough to distinguish the blazing fire that was now brewing in Evan.

"Um," Lana stumbled on the one syllable word while truthfully she wanted to run and hide, never be seen again, possibly even play Houdini and vanish into the log walls.

Nevertheless, Ches continued. "I do need to catch a ride out to my jeep though, so I can see if it needs any repairs. Lana said that it's still sitting in the woods. Do you know where Trey might be?"

"Why don't you just use your webbing and glide there?" Evan's tone was clipped.

Ignoring the sarcasm, Ches confusedly glanced between the two of them. "Whaddya mean?"

"What I mean, *spider man*, is that you can transform and be there in a matter of minutes if you use your webbing. Or, have you forgotten what you've become?"

The color drained from Ches's face as he sat back on the couch and placed his hands on each side of his head.

"You mean, it wasn't a dream?" He scratched the back of his neck. "I thought I was just knocked out or something."

"What an idiot," Evan grumbled as he headed for the kitchen. "Don't start having a melt down here. Wait until you get home. Then, you'll have the rest of eternity to cry over your misfortune."

"Evan Labonte!" Lana interjected, "That's not very nice."

"Well, I never claimed to be nice," he replied. "And, don't you think I've been nice enough by letting him sweat all over my couch for nearly a week, while I had to sleep sitting up in a chair listening to his moaning and groaning? Plus, while you two have been playing Romeo and Juliet, I've been out trying to get information on where your brother might be."

Lana was stunned. "You have? Is that where you've been all day?"

"Yeah," he nodded his head. "And, I think I may have a lead as to where he is."

"Oh, Evan!" Hurrying to him, she wrapped her arms around his waist. Then, she buried her face within his chest aiming to smolder the tears of joy that were burning at the back of her eyes. "Thank you! You don't know how much this means to me."

"Well, you could show me a little appreciation by getting lover boy outta' here. You have to remember, he's now an arachnid male and just the smell of him burns my nose and my blood.

And, having him sweating bullets in my house was nearly driving me to the point of suffocating him with my sock or burying a fork between his eyes. Believe me, I thought about it several times while I was trying to eat. His stench was killing me." Evan continued.

"Remember, Lana, you can't have two arachnid

males in the same territory, let alone the same house. Especially, when there's a female present. Look it up on the internet. I've done my research through the years. Two arachnid males will fight to the death over a female."

Ches sat forward and his brows rose with awareness. "So, what you're saying, Evan, is that we'll have to fight over Lana? And, with me now being a black widow spider, there's a good chance I could beat you."

Evan scoffed, "Not likely." His black iris voodoo returned, flashing with crimson-colored sparks of death. "If you challenge me, you'll definitely get hurt."

Ches quietly stood and glanced at Lana as he directed his comment to Evan, "Ya think so?"

Evan now glared at him. "I know so."

Ches's smile lit up the room. "Well, we'll see."

Their eyes remained locked as they heard Diana and Trey leaving the cabin next door and descending the steps. They listened in a discomforting silence as the two crossed the small patch of grass between the two cabins and headed in the direction to Evan's. Trey and Diana were softly chatting, quietly laughing as if they were old friends. They continued to chatter amongst themselves as they ascended the steps and knocked on the door.

"*Hello, is anyone in there*?" Diana sang out in her southern twang.

Neither Evan nor Ches were willing to tear their gaze away from the other. And, realizing they could be at this for hours, Lana stepped briskly to the front door and quickly opened it.

Diana was dressed in pale blue pajama bottoms and spaghetti string camisole. Her hair was piled high on her head and fashioned in a white ribbon; and, though her smile disappeared at the sight of Lana, she was still lovely. Diana pushed past her as if she hadn't seen her. She was dragging Trey along by the hand.

"So, what'rya' all up to?" she asked noticing the tension saturating the room.

Trey released Diana's hand. "Hey, I see you're up and around." And, embracing Ches, he happily patted him on the back. "Man, you had me scared there for a minute. I thought I had lost ya', buddy."

"You can't get rid of me that easy. Thanks for coming to my rescue."

"No problem, man. You call me any time you need me."

Trey then asked. "Did we come at a bad time? Diana had noticed that Evan was gone all day and thought we should come over and check things out."

Ches winked at Evan and grinned. "No. You didn't come at a bad time at all. We were just discussing some of the interesting things I'll be experiencing as an arachnid."

Evan balled his fists and the black iris voodoo returned.

Ches quietly laughed.

"Well, actually, you've come at a good time, Trey. I was wondering if you wanted to ride out with me to take a look at my jeep."

Trey looked at his friend in mild confusion. "Ya don't wanna' wait until morning when you can see a little better."

"Nah," Ches answered. "From what Evan here says, I'm now a black widow like him. So, I can see just fine in the dark. Remember, spiders have night vision. So, do ya' have your keys? I wanna drive."

"Sure." Trey pulled them from his pocket and tossed them to Ches who reflexively caught them. His eyes were still locked with Evan's.

"Nice catch," Trey remarked.

Tearing his gaze from Evan, Ches then walked to the front door and opened it. "You haven't seen anything yet."

Ches started Trey's car and put the shifter in reverse. Backing around, he headed in the direction of the forest and his jeep.

"Are you sure you're feeling okay?" Trey asked him. "I mean, you look like yourself now, but you were dead, deader'n road kill just a few days ago."

"I'm great. In fact, I've never felt better—more alive."

"Well, then, ya'd better put the headlights on. I don't want any more damage done ta my car. Evan already put a scratch along my bumper. He said he'd pay to have it fixed."

"Well, that was awfully nice of him. But, I won't dent your car. So, just sit back and relax."

Ches mashed his foot to the gas pedal and the car quickly fish-tailed and reached 60 mph. The darkened sky and black charger became one with the night as it raced along the dirt road in the direction of the river and forest.

Trey adjusted his eyes slightly to the darkness and watched as the enormous dark mass of forest quickly came into view. They were heading into the trees at 70 mph. Trey flinched and his heart nearly buckled within his chest.

"Holy shit!"

He white-knuckled the door handle and leather of the seat as he watched, through wide blue eyes, the trees coming at them in split-second intervals.

"Ches!"

"Relax, Trey. This is a piece of cake. Oh, and by the way—what have you been doing the whole time I've been sick?"

"You're asking me that now?" His eyes shot to his friend, afraid to leave the road for a second.

"Sure, why not? Now's as good as any."

"Um, let me think," his voice slightly quivered. "Well, I was sick for several days; and basically, Diana took care of me. Then, we just kinda hung out and talked, watched a few movies and waited for you to get better. Oh, and I did run back to the house to check on things and then I came back. Man, that chick Diana is a Goddess and she knows it. How she ever got mixed up with Evan is beyond me."

"I didn't notice. She's too bossy for me."

"Yeah, she is that."

Ches grinned. "So, are ya more relaxed?"

"Yeah, a little."

"Well then, I wanna see exactly what I'm capable of. So, let's have some fun."

Chapter 12

Ches climbed from the car, closed his door and looked around. He could see everything clearly as if it were day. Glancing back inside the window he waved a hand for Trey to come out.

"What'r'ya plannin' on doing, Ches?" Trey asked as he quietly slipped from the passenger's seat and stood next to the car. "I didn't think you'd be so enthused about all this. I mean things are going too fast and you have no idea how *you'll* personally react to the changes. I mean…" He paused and scratched the back of his neck. "Shit, I don't' know what I mean. I just think that this all has to do with Lana…Am I right?"

Ches just looked at him.

"I knew it. You're planning on going after the girl."

Silence spanned the space between them and Trey rubbed his hand over the roof of the car, like a mother stroking a child's head. His thoughts were rapidly traveling in several directions until he finally responded.

"Well, I don't think that'll settle too well with Evan; and, I think you're in for a real fight. However, no matter what you decide, buddy, I'm behind ya." His smile briefly lit the previously silent space.

Ches frowned. "No clichés'?"

Trey shrugged. "Can't think of any at this moment."

"Well, if you're finished braying like an over-protective mother mule can we concentrate on other things?"

"Well, I just wanted to get the technicalities outta the way. Just ta keep us on the same page."

Ches couldn't help but grin. "I always knew there was a reason I hung around you, because it certainly wasn't for your charm." He quietly laughed.

"Gee, I had always thought that's what it was; and here I find out it's something else." Trey laughed along with him. "So, now that we have all that cleared up, what's next?"

"I'm gonna climb up that tree." Ches pointed to a large locust tree just a few feet away. "Then, I'm gonna glide from that tree to that tree over there." His aim changed direction as he pointed to a tree another fifty feet away. "And, if I can't make it and fall, I want you to stand there…" His aim changed direction again. "And, catch me."

Trey laughed aloud. "No chance, buddy. You're on your own with that one."

"Thought so," Ches responded. "No. I want you to stay near the car; in fact, get in the driver's seat." Ches then disappeared into the darkness.

"What are you doing?" Trey called to him.

"I'm undressing. From what I remember Lana saying, we have to undress. Now, just stay in the car. I'll try not to hurt you."

"What?" Trey screeched as he hurried around the car, opened the door and slipped into the driver's seat, and then he rolled down his window. The nearby brush rustled lightly and he could hear Ches quietly moving around in the dark. A low moaning sound came from within the dark; it began to grow louder.

Shadows eerily rose and fell as the moon silently crept in and out from behind the clouds.

"Ches, Are you okay?" Trey opened his door to get out.

"Stay in the car!" Ches growled.

Trey quickly closed the door. "What's goin on?" He strained his eyes and watched as a massive shadow slowly moved amongst the trees and an ear-piercing screech ripped through the darkness.

Ches suddenly exploded into sight.

"Gah!" Trey jumped and caught his breath.

Ches was gigantic, somewhat larger than Evan, yet smaller than Spence. He tossed his head as his eight marble-like eyes darted erratically to and fro in the attempt to focus. And, shrieking, he opened his jaws which released the chattering sound made by his two billion teeth.

Slowly, Ches moved toward the car, his eight sinewy legs carrying him awkwardly across the forest floor. The air was still, quiet, an ominous calm which surrounded the area. Trey rolled his window up halfway as the giant beast stood staring at him through the glass.

"Ches? Can I come out?" There was no response, only the wild stare of the eight fanatic irises.

Trey grabbed his ball cap from the dash and placed it on his head. "Oh shit. All I'm gonna say is you'd better not eat me." Slowly, he opened his door and climbed out of the car.

Ches watched Trey closely, concentrating on his friend in the attempt to focus his eyes and keep his sanity. The initial pain of the transformation had disappeared and was replaced with an insurmountable amount of energy and strength. The need to run through the forest, to fight, eat, or glide through the air was overwhelming, awe-inspiring. All these feelings bombarded him in one tidal-wave of want; however, more than anything he desired at this moment, was for his friend to experience it with him. Without thinking, his webbing shot from his spinnerets and Trey was immediately encased to his neck within a cocoon.

"What the hell you doing, Ches?"

Ches yanked him to his large thorax; then, without warning, turned and bolted through the trees.

"Holy crap! Slow down!" Trey yelled as they plowed through the underbrush and passed one tree after another at a horrific speed.

The moon slowly slipped from behind the clouds, casting brief moments of light upon the forest floor below causing each shadow to become one menacing blur.

Ches suddenly came to an abrupt halt, quickly glanced around, then made for a nearby locust. Again, webbing shot from his spinnerets and he was immediately scurrying upwards.

Trey squeezed his eyes closed. "Oh, my God!" He could feel them ascending the tree. Higher and higher they climbed until they reached the top. Opening his eyes slightly, he looked around.

They were in the highest tree in the forest which overlooked the surrounding foothills and the woodlands which went on for miles. The moon was peaking through the layer of gray sky and streams of light played lightly upon the ground far below. The scene was poetic, beautiful.

"Wow, this is amazing," Trey caught himself staring out into the darkness, watching the gentle swaying of the surrounding forest as it moved within the breeze. The air was cool and crisp, invigorating to his senses; and, for a brief moment, he thought of his sister, Trisha, wondering if this was what a small taste of Heaven would be like.

Suddenly, Ches jumped from the limb where his eight legs had him secure.

"*Holy shit!*" The words tore from Trey's throat as he felt himself and Ches rapidly plummeting toward the ground. His adrenaline skyrocketed and he cried out again, "Oh my God! Ches!"

Webbing shot through the air and they were jerked skyward then propelled through the darkness toward another tree nearly 50 feet away. Ches grasped the tree tightly with his eight powerful legs then shot toward another branch nearly one hundred feet away.

Trey held his breath with each precise movement Ches made as he latched onto the next limb, plunged into the darkness then gracefully glided through the air. It was remarkable.

After an hour, they landed on the forest floor just a few yards from where the car was parked. Ches quickly released Trey from where he had him secured against him and tore through the cocoon with a swipe of his leg. He then immediately began to transform back into his human form. His breathing was labored as he dropped to his hands and knees and quietly shook his head.

"Hey, are you okay?" Trey asked as he steadied himself from the dizziness and brushed the remaining strands of webbing from his clothes.

"Yeah," Ches answered hoarsely. "Just a little outta breath."

"Well, what you did was amazing. I'm finding myself a little jealous."

"Don't be." Ches stood to his feet and talked as he headed in the direction of his clothes. "There are two things I need to do. One is to repay Spence for what he did to Lana. And, two is: get Lana to come home with me—beat Evan. Other than that, I could care less about all this spider nonsense." Turning, he looked back at Trey and smiled. "Though, that gliding is pretty awesome. Wouldn't ya say?"

Trey caught up to him and slapped him on the shoulder. "I'd say. That was great! However, I think I could enjoy the memory a little better if you were dressed. Your shiny derrière just ain't cuttin' it for me."

Ches playfully shoved him and disappeared into the brush. Seconds later, he appeared fully clothed.

"Let's head back."

"What about the jeep?" Trey asked.

"Ah, we'll just leave it till tomorrow. After all that sightseeing my derriere is just a little bit hungry." He glanced over at his friend. "And, I just don't think you'd taste very good."

Spence filled his arms with beer cans from the refrigerator and returned to the living room where his father, two brothers, Marty and Booger sat. He tossed each of them a can then sat down.

"So, what's so important, son?" his father asked as he popped the tab on the can, threw his head back and took a big swig. Releasing a loud belch, he took another swig and crushed the can within his hand.

"Yeah, Spence," Eddie added as he replicated what his father did. "Whadja call us out here for? Pop says that Colette's dead and you have somethin' you wanna show us."

“Colette’s dead?” Travis chimed in. “Shit! That’s too bad.” He grinned as he sat forward on the edge of the couch and licked his lips. His eyes seeped with excitement. “Sounds like we need to do us some ass-whoopin.”

“Yeah.” Spence observed the beer can within his hand as he rotated it to and fro. “Marty and Booger burnt the body out in the woods at the old Hobbs’ estate. That’s where she was killed.” He stopped turning the can, pulled the tab and drank its contents in one swallow.

“So, whaddya wanna do, Spence?” Marty asked. “We know who’s responsible for this.”

“Well, first off, I want everyone to come outside. I wanna show Pop, Eddie and Travis what we’re dealing with. Then, we need to come up with some sort of plan.” Spence stood up and walked toward the front door of the trailer.

“Uh…uh…, Spence,” Booger stood. All eyes were pasted on him. “I…I…think…I…might…be…be… able…to…help…”

Spence’s eyes became narrowed slits. He had been so preoccupied with getting revenge that he hadn’t noticed anything different about Marty or Booger when they had returned from the hospital, except the incessant stench of antibiotics and other pharmaceuticals that flooded his nostrils. But, as he now stood staring at Booger, he could smell the faint odor of Booger’s arachnid blood.

"So, you've tasted the blood, huh?"

Booger warily glanced up at Spence, uncertain as to how Spence would react.

"Was it the girl's?"

Booger responded with a slow nod of his head.

"Well, in that case, I want you to come outside and let's see what ya got."

"Damn, Booger! You sound like a girl." Eddie laughed and his father and Travis chuckled along with him. Booger's transformation was slow and painful. He screamed through nearly the entire process; and, when he was finished changing into his arachnid form, he was small, much smaller than even Colette had been.

"Holy shit! Is that cool or what?" Eddie stopped laughing and steadily backed away. Travis glanced over at his father who stood just feet away and their topaz-colored eyes locked.

"Son, I think ya might have somethin' here." A sadistic look glazed the yellow of his father's ice cold irises as he slowly made space between himself and the black widow beast.

"Ya ain't seen nothin' yet," Spence stood unmoving as he observed Booger's struggle within his arachnid form, knowing that if Booger were to get out of control and attack, he himself could transform and crush his friend like a bug.

Diana watched out her kitchen window as Trey pulled up in front of her cabin, got out of his car and waved to Ches who also got out and headed toward Evan's. It was just after midnight. Going to the front door, she opened it and stepped out onto the porch.

"Hey Ches, I don't know if ya'll be able to get in. I think they went to bed not long after ya'll left." She fingered a few curls that hung limply along her shoulders. "Ya'll are welcome to stay here if ya want."

"Nah." He waved her away. "Can't let Evan get too comfy on the couch." He quietly laughed.

"How'd ya'll know he was on the couch?"

He smiled. "I can hear him rustling around on the rough fabric. The recliner is leather and a bed is…well, you know…a bed is soft and has squeaky springs." With that, he turned and headed up the porch steps. Then, he knocked.

"Go away," he heard Evan grumble from inside.

"I can't. Trey has the only house key and has decided to stay here another night." Ches winked in Trey's direction.

"Then, why don't you just get it from him?" Evan asked.

Ches motioned for Trey to hurry into Diana's cabin. Trey tossed his hands in the air and quickly obeyed.

"Because he's already gone in and I don't wanna' wake Diana up."

Evan could sympathize with that. However,

his bare feet pounded along the wooden floor as he headed toward the front door. Within a few seconds he was flinging open the door and glaring at Ches.

"You sure are a pain in the…"

Lana appeared at the bedroom door. "Is everything okay?" She rubbed her eyes and yawned. "I thought I heard you yelling."

Ches quickly answered, "Everything's just fine." Pushing past Evan, he went to her side, gently put his arm around her shoulder and steered her back toward the bedroom. "Now, get some rest. We'll see you in the morning."

A low growl escaped Evan as he all but slammed the front door closed. Ches and Lana briefly stopped and looked at him.

"Evan, are you okay?" Lana asked.

"I'll be fine in the morning." Plopping into the recliner and crossing his arms, Evan laid his head back and closed his eyes. "I just need to get some rest, I was planning on getting some hours in at work tomorrow, then I wanted to get some more information on Samuel."

Lana couldn't help but smile inside as a warm feeling spread throughout her entire body. Leaving Ches's side, she went to Evan and quickly placed a kiss upon his forehead.

"Thank you."

His eyes opened. "You're welcome."

Lana grinned then happily spun around. "Good

night, Ches." Still grinning, she walked toward him and tenderly touched his arm. Then, she slipped inside the bedroom and closed the door behind her.

Ches stood there quietly watching her disappear out of sight.

Evan was playing dirty with the news of locating her brother; however, Ches knew how important it was to find Samuel. If he hadn't been laid up for the past several days, he would have been out searching too. Sighing, he turned and headed toward the couch.

Suddenly, Evan hopped from the leather recliner onto the sofa.

"I think I'll sleep here tonight." Switching off the light and closing his eyes, he folded his arms across his chest and nestled into the cushions to get comfortable. A large grin crossed his face. "Ah, nice."

Ches frowned and sank into the recliner; the sound of squishing leather momentarily drowned out the awkward stillness between them then stopped as he quit moving. A few minutes passed and then Ches spoke, "This isn't a race and Lana isn't a prize."

Evan glanced at Ches out of the corner of one eye. "Then, get outta the saddle and go home."

"Oh, I'm goin home all right and Lana may not come with me at first; but, I'm sure that eventually I'll change her mind. I won't give up—I love her too much."

"Well, I love her too."

"Is that why you left her?" Ches interrupted. "Left

her at my place, and all she did was cry for you for days?"

Evan thought about that for a moment. "If she was crying for me, then she must have been a mess from her transformation. You know she has a hard time controlling it."

"No, she did okay. All it took was a little comforting on my part—something you apparently don't possess. Too many years living as an arachnid beast has made you hard, insensitive to a female's thoughts and feelings."

A low growl involuntarily slipped from Evan's lips.

"Slow down, slow down. We have to handle this in a respectful manner—gentlemanly like." Ches chuckled. "Don't you agree?"

Evan didn't respond.

"I take it by your silence that means *no go.* Well then, let the best man win." Ches stuck his hand out toward Evan to shake. However, Evan pushed it away.

"I'm not shaking on anything with you, Romeo. The only shaking I'll do, will be ta shake the shit outta you."

Ches softly chuckled again. "Ya think so, Amigo. Well, like I said, 'May the best man win.'" With that he closed his eyes and drifted off to sleep.

Chapter 13

Evan leaned against the bathroom door with his arms crossed. He watched through his black iris voodoo Ches standing at the front door saying goodbye to Lana which was a little too friendly for his liking.

"Are you sure you have to go?" she asked Ches as he gently embraced her.

"Yes," he whispered into her hair, "or Evan and I may start butting heads."

"But, why do you two have to dislike each other?" A sadness filled her eyes.

Ches smiled his brilliant smile. "It's the nature of the beast. And, with such a lovely, warm, young female around it's hard to concentrate, let alone share." He softly laughed and his azure colored eyes twinkled. "You're making us crazy."

"But, I…" Ches placed a finger to her lips as he searched her melting eyes. "Sshh. You don't have to say anything. I'll be back." With that, he gently kissed her forehead. Then, he turned; and, without looking back, headed through the front door, down the steps and into Trey's car which sat idling out front.

Trey stared at his friend as he got in and closed the door. "Are you okay?"

"Not really," Ches responded. He glanced up to see Lana standing in the door watching him. She quietly waved and he smiled.

"I don't think I can live without her, especially now that I have some sort of creature lurking inside me that wants her more than anything." He looked over at Trey who was steering the car toward the dirt lane leading to where his jeep sat. "I don't know if you can fully understand that."

"I think I do," Trey slightly nodded. "And, what makes it even more difficult is that she reminds ya so much of Tricia."

"Yeah, somewhat," Ches agreed. "But yet, she's different, special in her own way."

Trey smiled. "Yeah, she is."

Lana closed the door. And, though the living room light was on, the cabin turned to darkness, confinement.

"Lana, are you sure this is what you wanna do, stay here?" Evan watched her expressions closely as she turned to face him.

"I'm sure," she responded. "I guess I just feel bad for some reason."

"Well, Ches and you are now bonded by blood." An ache rushed to his heart as he said it. "And, no matter what, you two will be bonded for eternity." He began to brood—hate the situation. He quickly had to think about something else to take his mind off what might occur; though, he did feel better since Ches was gone.

"Are ya hungry?" he suddenly asked as he made his way to the kitchen.

"No, I'm fine, thank you," she answered.

For the first time in days, they were alone and she suddenly became more aware of Evan's heartbeat, his blood temperature, his scent as it wafted through the remnants of air throughout the small cabin. She had forgotten its bouquet, while the house had been full of people with the various other smells they carried. Also, Ches's arachnid smell had been present, full within her nostrils. His scent was amazing; however, Evan's scent was intoxicating, like a drug she couldn't live without. For some reason, she suddenly felt parched.

"Evan..."

"Yeah," he responded from the kitchen.

"I'm really thirsty."

"What would you like to drink?"

Her first response was to answer, *Your blood, Evan. I want to drink your blood.* Suddenly, she felt foolish. What am I thinking? Was this something she could expect for the rest of her life—thoughts of drinking blood and bodily fluids? Yuck! The thought suddenly made her sick while her stomach was twisting in knots.

"I just need some water," she responded as she took a breath. He returned to her with glass in hand. Taking it, she guzzled it down.

Evan watched her; he could sense her arachnid beast which was causing her body temperature to increase and her sweat glands to mildly perspire.

Suddenly, she blurted out, "Evan, I'm scared. I don't know what's happening to me. I just had thoughts of drinking your blood!" She stared up at him.

Gently, he removed the glass from her trembling hand and placed it on the floor. He, then, took her into his arms; his words were warm within her hair like the rays of the morning sun that were now shining brightly upon their skin. "I know this is hard for you—all of this. Between losing your parents and not knowing how your brother is; and, then having to face the fact that you're no longer just Lana, but now something else, I'm surprised you haven't given up, or even, gone insane. But, somehow, we'll make it easier. I promise.

My thirst was different," he stated. "When I was first bitten, I craved blood and raw meat. It eventually passed, but, with a lot of coaxing from Grandmother Hobbs. She made me eat my hamburgers and steak cooked from the grill." He smiled warmly.

"Is she the woman in the picture on your dresser?"

Sadness filled his eyes. "Yes. She passed away a long time ago."

"I'm sorry." Lana was silent for a moment; then, she asked, "But, why am I craving your blood?"

His brows arched to his hairline. "Just mine? No-one else's?"

Lana knew immediately who he was referring to. Ches.

"No, no-one else," she replied.

"Well, if it's any consolation, I feel the same way about you," he remarked. His eyes sparkled like golden gems as he talked.

"Sometimes, I don't think I can stop myself. My arachnid's powers are strong. And, if the beast had its way, it would've feasted upon you a long time ago. But, I've been infected a long time; and, I wouldn't let that happen. That's one reason I'm afraid of Ches being around you. He's a newly born black widow, made by *your* blood; and, that makes him even more dangerous to you."

"But, I don't think he'd ever hurt me," she stated. "He's…," she paused as Evan pulled away.

"I'm not joking about this, Lana. Ches could really hurt you." He turned and began to walk away.

Lana grabbed him around the waist. "Evan, please… Please don't be angry." Pulling him close, she laid her head against his back. "Please."

Evan's already hard body was tense; and, his temperature from being around Ches still hadn't subsided. Spinning within her grasp, he pressed her to the wall. A mixture of emotions riddled his handsome features and his golden eyes welled with the same mixture of confusion and hurt.

"Lana, don't you understand? Don't you know why I feel the way I do…I love you. I've never had feelings like this toward anyone. *Anyone*. I've spent so many years alone in this miserable existence, wondering if

I would ever end up with someone who would fully understand or know me—love *me*. Now, you've come along and my emotions are driving me crazy; I can't stand the thought of you with someone else. And, whether it's my black widow that's fallen for you or just plain old me—I can't live without you..."

Suddenly, he pressed his lips against hers, drowning out his own words with the entanglement of their every breath. His mouth searched and tasted every bit of hers, moving gently, yet urgently, like a child tasting a multitude of ice cream flavors for the very first time.

His kiss was long and passionate, a whirlwind of heat and energy and Lana dug her fingers into the fabric of his shirt, tearing deep within his skin. He recoiled in pain, yet continued to cover every inch of her lips to her neck with slight, rhythmic motions of his mouth. And, entangling his fingers within her hair, he pulled her face closer, drawing upon her every breath.

Lana's head spun as her heart pounded within her chest and a tingling sensation raced from the back of her thighs to her spine. Suddenly, her legs buckled beneath her; however, Evan quickly swept her up into his arms and carried her to the couch. His lips broke from hers as he looked into her wide eyes.

"I can't let you go," he softly whispered as he placed her on the couch and lay on top of her. "I just can't."

Closing her eyes, she responded in a low winded

breath, "Then, don't."

His body pressed against her as he kissed her again. Every muscle within him was hard; and his normally cool skin was now burning hot. Lana knew this was what she wanted; she wanted him. His lips pulled from hers and she slowly opened her eyes.

"Lana…do you love *me*?"

"Yes," she replied through a breath. Her lips searched for his. "I love you more than anything." She closed her eyes again.

Suddenly, he was sitting up and sliding away from her.

Her eyes immediately opened. "What's wrong?"

Evan looked over at her. Her hair was wild and her clothing was a mess. He watched as her eyes flashed from the deepest walnut brown to the brightest crimson red: He imagined his were doing nearly the same.

Webbing slowly streamed from her black widow mark; she was beginning to change, somehow look different. It was her arachnid coming alive; and, that wasn't good.

If he and she were to take their relationship to another level as human beings, what would that mean for each of their beasts? Would he be able to control the animalistic urges enough not to kill her? Of course, he wearily stated to himself. He had been around other females and hadn't transformed. However, Lana was a *black widow* female and his inner beast craved her like no other. Or, would it be just the opposite where the female black widow, after mating, ate the male?

He cleared his throat which felt to be slightly restricted; and, sliding her legs, which had been entangled around him to his lap, he regretfully stated, "We have to stop."

"No. Why?" Lana asked as she sat up. "Did I do something wrong? I've never done anything like this before." Her eyes were no longer brown, but, now a blazing crimson while her arachnid form was definitely spiraling to the surface, begging to come alive.

"No, you didn't do anything wrong."

Taking her hands which were clutching at his shirt, he gently kissed each one. "I just don't want to endanger you by causing your transformation. It was bad enough you had to do it for Ches."

"No," Lana interrupted as she pulled him back toward her. "It'll be okay." She buried her face within his neck and kissed him tenderly, softly; while her body was numb, yet weighted, as she pressed herself against him wanting him more now than ever. She had never felt this way about anyone before—had never even been kissed.

A picture of Diana unexpectedly entered her mind. Its image burned upon her intellect, made it nearly impossible to think. Diana's perfect body was pressing against Evan and she was kissing him, kissing him hard. Anger immediately welled within Lana's beast and she pulled Evan closer—possession of the male arachnid controlling her now.

"Evan..." she spoke into his ear. Her breath was warm, flowery. "I want you to do to me, what you've done to Diana, to other girls. You said you loved me."

Every touch and breath made Evan weak and desire rushed throughout his body urging him to gather her up and make them one. His mind was becoming clouded and he knew she was beginning to use her powers on him.

"Lana..." he breathed, "Stop." Her lips slipped from his ear and locked with his mouth; and, as her tongue lightly touched his teeth, his arachnid beast sparked to life. The energy within him soared, nearly driving him to insanity.

With every ounce of human strength, he pulled away and leapt to his feet.

"No. We have to stop."

"What's wrong?" she asked. Her eyes blazed red—flashed between anxiety and irritation—the beast within her was on the rise.

He pointed to where her sweater had slightly ridden up her stomach. "Look at your mark—the hourglass mark near your navel. You're changing, Lana. Your black widow is trying to control you *and* me. I don't want to do this as inhuman beasts. I've had enough of that. If this is going to happen, then I want it to be as humans—man and woman."

Lana quietly rose from the couch, moving as a cat on the prowl. Her flaring gaze was wild, mesmerizing as she stared up into his eyes and pressed herself against him.

"Please, Evan."

Within seconds, her webbing was pouring from her tattoo and quickly wrapping itself around him, drawing their bodies tautly together so their faces were inches apart. Her fiery red lips reached for his, kissing him passionately while she had become someone or *something* else—exactly what Evan had feared.

Lana's hands slid beneath his shirt and her fingers ran lightly along his back. Then, she quietly slipped them into the back of his pants and pressed him against her. Her red eyes were locked to his.

Evan's head spun out of control; and, he now knew that Lana's arachnid beast had caught him within its mesmerizing stare—he would soon become her prey.

"Lana…you have to stop." He could hear the female black widow calling to the male, a song of seduction, a baited trap to make him love her and bring him to the height of ecstasy. Then, when his energy was spent and his body weak, she would feast upon him as a succulent meal.

A breathless scream rushed from her parted lips and she bit back the pain as her eight legs tore through the flesh of her back and burst through her sweater. Quickly, her legs latched on to Evan—four securing him, while four lightly hovered over his body, touching all areas of his exposed skin. She had partially transformed.

“Lana.” Her name became no more than a choked whisper as he saw two elongated fangs suddenly push through her upper gum. Her eyes were swirling within their blood-colored sockets when suddenly all eight legs latched onto him and the two fangs tore into his throat.

“Ugghh!” He screamed in pain as his arachnid beast could no longer come alive—protect him from her deadly advances, while the two bloody fangs rapidly drew back and ripped into his throat again.

Poison pumped into Evan’s system sending a burning sensation rushing throughout his body: he knew he wouldn’t last very long.

For what seemed an eternity, Lana remained with her fangs lodged deep within Evan’s neck. She tasted of his blood, the sweet nectar that only he possessed as her female black widow needed him sedated, wanted him weak so she could do with him as she wished.

Suddenly, her attention was caught by something—something close by. A deep, sinister hiss rolled from her throat as her fangs extracted and her head whipped in the direction of the door.

Chapter 14

"What the heck you doin', Lana?" Diana suddenly stopped in her tracks as she watched Evan, wrapped partially in Lana's cocoon, drop to the floor. Lana's eyes blazed and stared at her viciously, like a female panther protecting its prey.

"Oh, my God! What did ya'll do to him?" Diana stepped toward Evan, however, she was immediately cut off as Lana quickly placed herself between them.

"Get out," the vicious command seeped from behind jutting fangs.

Diana took a step backward as she glanced around the room for something she could use as a weapon.

"No. I'm not leaving Evan here. Ya'll are tryin' ta' kill him." Diana caught her breath as Lana lunged in her direction. And, whirling on her heels, she rushed for the open door.

Suddenly, she crashed onto the front stoop. Lana was on her back.

"Stay away from Evan," Lana hissed.

Fear slightly reverberated in Diana's voice as she cried back, "No, I won't! I'll kill ya'll before I'll let ya'll have him." She fought to get away; however, Lana's webbing was quickly encasing her.

A loud screech tore through Diana's ears and she screamed as Lana's fangs suddenly tore along her skin.

"Lana!"

Suddenly, Diana could hear Evan's voice.

"Lana! Stop!"

Evan quickly plucked Lana's slender body into the air.

Lana struggled and fought, continued to hiss at Diana as Diana, using her arms and hands, scrambled away.

Evan, immediately, placed his hand over Lana'a eyes so she couldn't use her arachnid powers on him again. Briefly, she struggled; then, suddenly, she became subdued. Her body went limp within his arms and removing his hand, he carried her in and laid her on the couch.

Then, without looking Lana's way, he headed back to help Diana. Quickly, he tore the webbing from her body; however, his hand was pushed away when he attempted to help her to her feet.

Fury burned in Diana's eyes which were beginning to fill with tears. She looked at him and angrily asked, "Ya'll would choose *that*, over me?" Then, quickly spinning, she ran down the steps, across the yard to her cabin and disappeared inside.

Evan could hear her sobs from where he stood. He felt awful, guilty, like he had done something wrong; however, right now he couldn't fix the situation between them. He needed to take care of things here first.

Slowly, he closed the door and turned his attention

back to Lana who was now also crying. Then, rubbing the puncture wounds on his neck, he walked over and sat down next to her on the couch.

"Oh, my God," the words were choked through her tears. "I'm so sorry." Her body trembled uncontrollably.

Evan quickly wrapped his arms around her and pulled her to his chest.

"Ssh. It's okay." He gently stroked her hair.

"No. No, it's not," she blubbered into his shirt. "I can't believe how I acted and what I did." She hurriedly added, "But, I couldn't stop." Her teary gaze caught his. There was no longer a beast that was hiding behind her chocolate-colored irises, but now the warm, sweet girl he loved.

"Evan, please…don't ever let me turn into that again. Please—not ever. I'd rather be dead than be that horrible creature that just hurt you and hurt Diana. Plus, I just acted like…"

He cut her off. "It's okay. I promise."

She wept for several long minutes as he gently stroked her back and hair and continuously checked for any sign of her arachnid legs. Surprisingly, they had disappeared after he had pulled her off Diana and covered her eyes. He thought it rather strange. Her arachnid couldn't have been subdued by just covering her eyes. He had only done that so she couldn't control him. Had her energy been so depleted by the creature that she couldn't transform now? He wondered. And, how was her energy fueled or brought to an end? She was crying now and her legs and webbing weren't anywhere to be seen.

After a few minutes, Lana's crying subsided and he released her. "You never have to apologize for what you can't control." Then, looking into her eyes, he said, "Hey, how about we get outta' here, spend the day doing something fun. And, while we're out, I'll try and get some more information on Samuel."

"Well, what about Diana? I need to go and apologize. Plus, I thought you had to work today?" She ran the back of her hand across her eyes and sniffled.

"As far as Diana is concerned, that'll have to wait till later. She needs to cool down a little first. And, I can take care of the work I need to do while we're out. It'd be a quick job and then we can leave. Do you mind hanging out for a little, while I work? You could watch?" His brows rose to his hair.

"Yeah, that would be nice. What kind of work do you do?"

"Construction," he replied, then motioned with his fingers, "high end jobs."

A meek smile crossed her lips. "I bet you're the best."

He smiled. "That's what they say." He then glanced at her clothing; they were splattered with blood and her top was shredded by her partial transformation. "Are those the only clothes Diana gave you?"

Lana nodded her head.

"Well, we'll just have to take you shopping. What kinds of clothes do you like?"

Lana shrugged. "I guess anything that doesn't make me look fat or fifty."

Evan softly laughed. "Lana, I don't think there's anything that could ever make you look fat. I just plucked you into the air with one hand. What are you—five, three, maybe…" He slowly eyed her up and down, "…one twelve?"

Playfully, she smacked him. "That's one-o-five, buster." Her mood was steadily brightening.

Evan laughed and pulled her close; and, looking into her big brown eyes, he gave her a kiss. It was gentle, sweet; while, what had just occurred, was still too fresh in their minds. Quickly releasing her, he grabbed her hand and pulled her from the couch.

"Come on; let's find you something to wear." He led her into the bedroom; and, searching through a few drawers of his dresser, he produced a pair of pink shorts and a black turtleneck. "Here, you can wear these." He handed her the articles of clothing.

"Are they Diana's?" Lana inquired uneasily, her stomach sinking as she asked.

Evan was busying himself by searching through the back of his armoire. He produced more clothing, various articles that may have been worn by a teenage girl.

"I forgot they were here," he remarked.

Thinking that he hadn't heard her, Lana asked again. "I guess they're Diana's?"

Evan quickly glanced her way. "No. They're not Diana's."

They walked in silence toward the back of the cabin and started on a path that headed into the woods.

"Where are we going?" she asked.

"It's a surprise." Evan glanced over at her and winked as if the earlier situation hadn't occurred.

"Evan…"

"Yeah?"

Lana paused and looked over at him, unsure of how to approach him about the clothing. She figured he had been with other girls throughout his long life, had probably even done more with them than just kiss. However, now she was with him and couldn't even do that without wanting to suck his blood or kill him. Her heart ached at the thought, ached terribly at the mere idea of him being with anyone else.

Glancing down at the top and shorts, she ran her hand along their fabric. The top was cashmere, good cashmere and the shorts were a good quality. Evan was so good looking, she was sure the female who had worn these must of been beautiful. She had to be.

"What's the matter, Lana? Is it the clothing?"

He stopped and looked at her. His golden eyes were warm and considerate; their flecks of gems sparkled like diamonds in the morning sunlight. He was just too gorgeous.

"...Did you love the other girls?" she quietly asked.

A soft laugh escaped his perfect lips and his eyes narrowed. "Is that what all this is about?"

"Well..." she stammered in embarrassment.

"Look..." He pulled her toward him and looked deep within her troubled eyes. "...I love you; and only you." And, kissing her again on the forehead, he led her by the hand to a path behind the cabin.

Within several minutes, a small brown shed came into view. It was hidden deep in the woods several hundred feet away. Evan stopped in front of it and pulled a key from within his jeans pocket and slid it into the padlock. Jimmying the lock open, he pushed back the doors. They screeched in protest as they ran along their dirt-ridden tracks, then Evan stepped inside.

The shed was dark; however, Lana was still able to see.

Evan worked quickly to remove a large tarp from what was occupying the center of the floor. She inhaled at what she saw.

It was a motorcycle; one like she had often seen on the highway passing her mom and dad at what seemed 100 mph. It was metallic black with glistening silver chrome and a small black widow emblem embossed on the gas tank.

"Wow, that's so cool," she stated."

Evan grinned. "Ya like it?"

"Who wouldn't?" she remarked, as she walked over and ran her hand lightly over the shiny gas tank. "Is it yours?"

"Yep," he smiled crookedly and winked. "One of the items I purchased with the money Grandmother left me."

"Grandmother Hobbs left you the money?"

The grin disappeared from Evan's face and was again replaced with a visible sadness. "Yeah, when she passed away."

"I'm really sorry," Lana gently touched his arm. "I know you had mentioned it before."

"It was a little over thirty years ago. You'd think I'd be over it by now."

Lana cocked her head to the side. "So, you didn't know her? She died before you were born?"

Evan laughed. "No, she was the one who helped me when I was little. Marianne Hobbs, Diana's great grandmother. She was the one who raised me."

Lana was even more confused. "She raised you? So, how can that be if she passed away nearly thirty years ago?"

Evan's brows rose to his hairline as he walked around the bike and embraced her. "You don't know do you? You don't know how old I am?"

Her nose scrunched up and her brows furrowed

as she studied his face. "Well," she finally answered after a moment, "I would say you're about eighteen going on nineteen; but, somehow, I think you're going to say something different. Please don't tell me you're like 12,000 years old. That would just be creepy."

Wearily, he studied her face, especially her eyes. "So, my age would change things between us?"

"No. I don't think so," she responded. "Though, it would be kind of strange telling people that I like a boy who's older than Ramses."

Evan interrupted. "No. I'm definitely not that old—more like, I was able to see them test drive the first automobile. That was kinda neat—everyone was so excited. It was the big thing back then." He smiled sheepishly.

"Oh my God!" Lana stared into his face. "Wasn't that near the 1900s?"

"1908 to be exact," Evan corrected her. "That's when Henry Ford invented the Model-T."

"Gee, aren't we intelligent," she teased.

"Well, I've had enough time to learn some things; but, not quite everything." He grinned. "So, quit avoiding the question: How old do you think I am?"

Lana wormed her way out of his grip and stood with her hands on her hips eyeing him from head to toe. "Hmm," she gently poked the skin on his arm then his chest. They were both firm, nearly rock hard. "According to the texture of your petrified skin," she grinned. "I'd say you're about…"

"Hey, Whaddya mean petrified skin." He rubbed the skin on his arm. It felt like normal skin to him.

She laughed and her smile seemed to light up the entire forest. Evan laughed along with her. Then, they stopped and the surrounding area became still.

"I'm 108," he quickly stated.

"Wow, you're 108?"

A slight sadness filled his eyes as he seemed to be contemplating the number of years he had been alive. "Yep; and, today is my birthday."

"It's your birthday today? I didn't know that." Suddenly, she became quiet. "I wasn't able to get you anything. I'm sorry."

"Hey, it's okay. Don't worry about it."

"No. That's not right. You have to get something on your birthday."

"I always do," he softly laughed. "Diana always made sure of that. That's probably why she was over. Welp…" he raised his brows and made a face. "I guess she'll be over tomorrow."

"I just bet she will." The words had slipped from Lana's lips before she could stop them. Quickly, she turned her back toward him.

"Hey," he gently wrapped his arms around her waist and spoke into the back of her dark hair, "you have to be careful. You could've really hurt her today."

"I know; I'm sorry. I'll have to apologize to her. But, for some reason, the black widow within me hates her, can't stand her coming around."

"Yeah," he agreed. "That's how it is with me, especially when Ches is around. Then, it's really bad." He smiled apologetically then shrugged. "I guess we're just bound to stay together as two green-eyed monsters."

Then, he quickly released her. "Welp, are ya ready to take a ride?"

"My mother would hate you for this. She absolutely abhorred motorcycles. And, don't we need any helmets?"

"I don't have any. When the helmet law changed, I tossed mine; well, not exactly, I gave it to some kid near the work site in town. But, I never needed one. And, if it makes you feel any better, *Spider Woman*, you shouldn't need one either." Touching her nose with his forefinger, he grinned.

She smiled meekly, then asked, "Will *I* live to be 108; and, will I look as young as you. Or, am I going to age and die like someone normal, someone who isn't a black widow? And, what about Ches? What'll happen to him?"

Evan's thoughts quickly raced to Ches being hit by a train; though, unfortunately, that probably wouldn't kill him. He sighed, then turned his attention back to Lana who was anxiously awaiting an answer.

"I imagine you'll live a long time, maybe to be *two hundred* and eight." He smiled warmly. "But, I can't guarantee anything. Colette lived as an arachnid for a very short time, but that was because Trey decapitated her. I was shot several times and stabbed several times; however, each time the beast within me rejuvenated me, brought me back and slowly healed me. Spence was hit by a tractor trailer, which I wish would happen to Ches." His eyes cut to her to see her response.

"Hey! That's not very nice." Lana elbowed him in the stomach and he doubled over laughing at her reaction. Then, he grabbed at her sides to tickle her.

Giggling, she then spun and stomped her foot. "Stop! I'm serious now. I wanna know if I'm going to grow old alone or if I'm gonna stay young?"

His brows arched and his forehead creased as he thought about it. Then, he responded, "I'm sorry; I don't have all the answers. However, there is one thing I do know: I know that I care a lot about you, more than anyone I've ever known, even Grandmother Hobbs. But, she was more like a mother to me, so I guess that really doesn't count—then, of course my actual mother and father, from what I remember of them, I loved them too."

Slipping his arms around her, he stared into her eyes. "I will promise you this, though: If it takes every breath I have to keep you alive and safe, I'll do it—no matter what."

Lana laid her head on his chest and quietly spoke, "But, I don't wanna grow old without you. You'll probably stay young and I'll look like a dried up old prune. You wouldn't even wanna know me then. You'd go off with some beautiful girl who looked like she was about seventeen or eighteen."

Evan softly chuckled. "You worry too much. No matter what, I'd still like you."

"Ah ha!" She pointed a finger at him. "So, you would just *like* me—like a grandma!"

"No," he laughed, "a little more than that."

"How much more?" Her eyes became narrowed slits as she studied him closely.

"I'll let ya know then." He smiled wickedly and winked. Then, letting her go, he turned and began to steer the motorcycle out the shed doors and onto the graveled patch of stone in front of the shed.

"Hey, that's not fair."

"Who ever said that anything in life was fair?" he remarked as he climbed onto the bike. Then, he turned and asked, "Are ya coming?"

"No. You never answered me." She stood with her arms crossed and her feet planted.

"Suit yourself." He twisted the key, pressed the start button and began to pull away. Then, he stopped and lazily turned on his seat. "I'll give you an answer if you get on."

Grinning his perfect grin, he patted the leather seat behind him. "Come on, it's my birthday, enough talk about old age; let's go have some fun."

Lana couldn't help but be captivated by his smile. "Ya promise?"

He answered, "I do."

Chapter 15

Lana climbed on the back of the motorcycle. It wobbled slightly and she quickly grabbed onto Evan's shirt.

"Oh my God!"

"What's the matter?" he asked.

"I've never been on a motorcycle before. Is it safe?"

He chuckled softly. "This coming from a girl who can knock down trees. Just wrap your arms around my waist and hold on tight. I promise you its safe. Oh, and when I lean, you lean the same way."

The bike slowly moved and Lana wrapped her arms tight around his waist, forgetting about the answer she had been so adamant about receiving earlier. *Besides, it could wait until later*, she thought.

They continued on the path through the forest, in the opposite direction of the cabin. After a few moments, they reached a macadam road which displayed a sign stating twenty-five miles to Aune'.

"This is the way I go to work," Evan stated. "I have to take the bike or people would start asking questions."

They reached a higher speed and the motorcycle buzzed along the road. The morning air was fresh and clean; it blew upon Lana's face and through her hair. Smiling, she squeezed Evan tighter and laid her head upon his shoulder. In no time, they were at the construction site.

Evan pulled to the side of the road and turned the bike off. The ride had ended too quickly.

"Welp, here we are." Evan planted his feet on the ground and waited for Lana to climb off, then he pulled his leg over and quickly dismounted.

"Now that wasn't so bad, was it?" He grinned.

"No." She smiled back. "It was kinda' neat!"

"Good. I'm glad you liked it. We'll take a longer ride after I get finished here."

"Whaddya have'ta do?" she asked.

Evan waved a hand at two workers as he and Lana got closer to the work site. It reminded Lana of a small group of ants she had once seen in their back yard who were busy transporting a piece of apple either she or Samuel had dropped earlier to a nearby anthill. That was the same case now. Dozens of men were scurrying around in an attempt to finish the massive bridge they were constructing that ran between Aune' and the city of Bridgeton which sat on the other side of the mile wide canal.

Hammers banged against metal and various types of drills and machinery were filling the air with their barrage of ear-piercing screeches and groans.

For a brief moment, Lana covered her ears waiting for the loud ringing to stop, until she could tone down her heightened sense of hearing to a minimal level. This would take some practice and getting used to. It didn't seem to bother Evan—more than likely from his many years of having to adjust.

Lana glanced over at him as he waved to someone else; then, he led her toward a small trailer that sat a few hundred feet from the worksite. *Over one hundred years old*, she thought. *He sure does look good for being over one hundred years old.*

They ascended the few rickety steps that led up into the trailer; Evan rapped twice, then entered. A strong scent of strawberry raced from inside and Lana sneezed.

Two large desks occupied the small area inside with an overstuffed file cabinet and several cardboard boxes that were stacked in a far corner. Each desk had someone sitting at it. One was a middle aged woman with a slightly round center, wearing a pair of excessively tight polyester shorts and a button up blouse; and, the other was a young girl just a little older than Lana with short red hair. Each glanced up and smiled wide at the sight of Evan; however, the younger female's features darkened noticeably at the sight of Lana coming in behind him.

Both females chimed out a, "Good morning," to Evan, then the older female handed him a slip of paper.

Evan glanced at it and slipped it into his pants pocket. Then, he plopped down in a burgundy-colored recliner in front of the younger girl's desk and instructed Lana to sit in an identical chair next to him.

"Where's Bob?" Evan asked her.

Ignoring Lana, she leaned forward on her elbows

and placed her chin in her hands. Her long lashes batted several times at him as if she were using Morse' Code'. "He's on his way in. Wants to talk to you about what he needs done today. Says you can meet him out at the site." Smiling, she displayed perfect white teeth, which made her very attractive.

"Well then, I guess I'd better be heading out. I'll see you ladies later." Evan stood and motioned for Lana to follow. When he took her hand, the Green-eyed Dragon—jealousy—made an appearance on the young girl's face. The girl's phone rang and her eyes darted toward it in annoyance; then, she quickly picked up the handset.

"Hello, Hobbs' Construction. This is Angie speaking. May I help you?" Smiling at Evan, she spun in her chair and went back to work. Lana and Evan left the trailer and headed for the work site to meet the construction foreman, Bob.

"So, I guess Angie was kinda upset about me being with you," Lana remarked as she and Evan walked side by side.

"What makes ya say that?" Evan softly laughed. "I thought she kinda liked you." He grinned.

"Yeah, kinda like for me to fall off a cliff or something. Have you two ever gone out?"

"Yes," he remarked, "out to lunch every time we move to a new site."

Lana stopped in her tracks. "Were you boyfriend and girlfriend?" She could feel her heart cracking at the thought.

His face scrunched up as he thought about it. “No. Things didn’t work out. She’s really not my type.”

“Well then…what is your type?” she lightly stammered. They began to walk again.

Evan stopped short and looked at her, then touched her nose again. “Why…you are.” He smiled his perfect smile and started in the direction of where he would be meeting the construction foreman.

Lana grinned from ear to ear, certain that the dozens of people busy at work had stopped just to stare at her mouth pasted in a ridiculous half moon across her face. She didn’t care. This was the best she had felt in quite awhile and she would savor the moment. However, there wouldn’t be much time for romance and dating; that would have to wait until after they found Samuel.

The construction platform was separate from where the other workers were working by a huge mound of dirt and a small patch of trees. In a few minutes, they were out of sight of the others and could see Bob waiting on the concrete platform just beneath the monstrous-sized construct that was going to be part of the bridge.

He was a large man in his mid-fifties with a precisely trimmed beard and mustache. However, compared to the colossal-sized steel structure above him, he appeared no more than another ant.

Lana had never realized just how big sections of

bridges were. They were gigantic. And, though she was completely amazed, for some unknown reason, she suddenly had the urge to climb it.

"Good morning, Evan." Bob's thick hand shot out to shake Evan's. Then, he turned to Lana and asked, "So, who's the young lady you have with you today?"

Evan smiled and answered, "This is Lana."

The large hand then shot in her direction. "Nice to meet you, Lana."

Quickly, he turned and his demeanor was all business. "This is what we need you to do." He pointed to the top of the structure. "There's a hairline crack in the farthest elbow. An aerial news craft caught sight of it as they were broadcasting a special on the fishing tournament being held in the canal two miles south of here. I don't know if its luck, or a curse for us that they saw it. Because, now it'll be spread all over the six o'clock news letting everyone know of our incompetence. However, we certainly wouldn't want any incidences in the future where someone would get hurt. All I know is that it needs to be fixed pronto and you're the only guy who can do the job.

The welder's over by my truck, along with anything else you'll need. I don't know how you'll do it, and according to Mr. Hobbs, you've been doing this for a long time and I'm not supposed to ask questions. Anyway, just get the job done. Then, check in with Angie to give a report, and Marge will have your pay.

Welp, I have some work to do myself." Shielding

his eyes from the sun, he looked up to the highest point of the structure. Then, he looked at Evan and chuckled. “I certainly wouldn’t wanna be in your shoes. However, good luck.”

Turning, he walked toward his truck, climbed in and drove away.

Lana shielded her eyes as she stared up at the gargantuan steel figure. Her eyes slightly watered. Then, she looked at Evan in disbelief.

“You’re going to go way up there?” She pointed to the farthest elbow. “And, do what? Welding? Are you insane?”

Evan softly laughed. “Piece of cake. But, it’s gonna get hot today—Indian Summer ya know. So, I don’t wanna be up there long. Arachnids aren’t sunbathers.” He walked toward the welder and called to her over his shoulder. “So, are ya coming?”

“What, over there?” Lana asked.

“No, silly, up there.” He pointed to the spot at the top of the structure where he was to do the welding.

“What? You want me to go up there with you?”

“Sure. Don’t you have the slightest urge?”

“Well, yes…some,” she admitted. “But, how did you know that?”

“Because,” he looked directly into her eyes, “we are alike. And, the first moment I laid eyes on one of these structures, I couldn’t wait to race to the top. Of course, that was ages ago; and back then, around the hippy era, the bridges were lower and everyone had just thought I was strung out on acid or something when they saw me climb them.

Luckily, for me the police didn't come. That's the last thing I would have needed." He paused for a moment.

"You know, I don't exist, don't you? There are no records of me anywhere: I never went to school; was educated by my grandmother; never paid taxes; and, don't even have a social security card, driver's license or bank account."

His smile waned. "If anything would've happened to me, no-one would've even known or cared—except, of course, for Diana."

"So, then how do you drive and cash checks and all that?" Lana quietly asked.

"Well, I drive without a driver's license and I never have to cash checks. I always get paid with cash. And, Grandmother had it stated in her will that I was to have employment in the Hobbs' family business as long as they were around. So, here I am; and, here you are."

"Well, doesn't anyone ever notice that you haven't aged?"

He laughed. "Yeah, all the time. But, I just tell them that its genetics—I tell them that both my parents looked like they were twelve. You should see some of the looks I get."

His smile reappeared and he changed the subject as he glanced up at the structure. "Well, are you up for the challenge?"

"I don't know."

"I'll tell you what: I'll take the welder up and get it set up. Then, I'll come back down and get you. How about it? I promise you, you'll love it. And, isn't there just a hint of curiosity inside that head of yours?" He touched her forehead with his finger.

"I guess," she finally answered.

"All right, then. Let's get going." Shoving a pair of gloves in his back pocket and heaving the heavy welder onto his back, which would have normally taken the strength of three men to lift, he started for the structure. "I'll be right back."

Within a matter of minutes, he was hoisting himself by rope up the side of the steel configuration; and, after a short time he reached the top. He looked small, merely a tiny child against the background of the enormous structure and the mammoth sized sky. Lana could see his tiny arm waving, then suddenly; he was leaping into the sky and racing toward the ground.

"Oh my God! Evan!" Her hands shot to her chest as she froze. Then, forcing her limbs to move, she ran toward the structure. "Noooo!"

Suddenly, Evan began to transform in mid-air. However, only two of his legs burst from his back as his webbing shot out before him. And, spinning about several times, he landed with a thud to his feet. Then, as quickly as his arachnid legs appeared, they disappeared.

Taking a deep breath, he walked toward her.

"Oh my God! You dummy! You nearly gave me a heart attack!" She smacked his arm when he reached her. "You scared me to death."

Evan softly laughed. "Yeah, you should have seen your expression when I jumped." He laughed louder. "I zoomed my sights right in on your face. Your mouth flew open and your eyes were as large as coconuts."

"Stop. It's not funny. I thought you were gonna die." Spinning around, she crossed her arms and stared in the opposite direction.

Evan quit laughing and gently wrapped his arms around her. "I'm sorry." He kissed the top of her head. "That's the only thing I like about being a black widow—jumping from high places. And, I didn't think you would get so upset. "Again, I'm sorry. Will you forgive me?"

Lana twisted around to face him. His puppy-dog eyes were pleading and he bore a jutting lower lip.

Her eyes turned to narrowed slits. "Only if you promise never to do that again in front of me."

Evan grinned as he made a sign of the cross on his chest. "I promise. Now, are ya ready to go up? That sun's gonna be murder in an hour or so and I wanna be done by then."

"Okay. I guess I'm ready." Worry stretched across her face as she attempted a smile.

"Well, then just put your arms around my neck

and hold on tight."

Lana did as she was told and Evan wrapped his left arm which was like granite, snuggly around her. Then, bolting toward the metallic strands of webbing that stretched from one steel beam to another, he jumped and grasped onto them.

"Hang on!" he shouted. Then, quickly shoving his free hand and feet within the webbing, he swiftly raced along the strands and ascended the silk threading like a ladder.

Lana closed her eyes, and after a few seconds, they had reached the top.

Chapter 16

"You can open your eyes now." Evan stated as he slowly released Lana and slid his hand within hers. He held onto it tightly.

"Well, whaddya think?" His smile was brilliant, alive. She could tell that he loved this and she was awfully glad to be a part of it.

Opening her eyes was like seeing the sky for the very first time. No words could describe it. Various hues of blue surrounded them, complimented by the white of the cotton-candy clouds that drifted gently overhead. A light breeze was blowing, making the air seem cooler, crisper. It was amazing.

"Well?" he asked, "Isn't this great!" With no response, he bent to look into her face. "Lana? Are you okay?"

Her eyes blinked as she smiled and her words were but a whisper. "It's fantastic. I don't even know how to describe it."

Slowly, she moved her feet along the beam which was no more than three feet wide; and, when she glanced down, her head spun.

"Whoa!" She grabbed Evan's arm with two hands. "I guess my balance and human fear of heights still exists."

"Probably, so don't look down. And, maybe you

should sit while I'm working. It'll only take me a few minutes to seal this crack up; then, we can leave."

"Okay."

With Evan's help, she awkwardly got to a sitting position and hung her legs over the side. "Wow, this is amazing."

"I told you so," he remarked as he grabbed a brush and began to clean the crack of any debris. Then, putting on the gloves, goggles and a welder's hood, he turned on the welder, adjusted the torch, and went to work.

"Don't look at the flame," he shouted above the hammering vibration of the welder. "It could hurt your eyes, especially since they're so sensitive now."

"Okay," she called back, "I won't."

The sun was rising, an enormous ball of yellow haze which sat along the horizon to the east. It warmed her face, though stung her eyes as she stared at its massive form. She stretched her arm out as if to touch it, feel its warmth through her fingertips. Then, shaking her head and rubbing the back of her hand across her eyes, she looked out over the roving hills and mountains, across the water and over to Bridgeton.

Bridgeton was a large city, with towering skyscrapers and numerous highways that were shaped like bow ties. For the average human, the city sat far away, silent, quiet; however, for Lana, it was a barrage of sights and sounds, a large playground for its many occupants. The desire to see more was overpowering, riveting.

Smiling, Lana narrowed the sights of her highly developed vision and watched and listened. The mild hum of construction, machinery, and vehicles on the move, drifted through the warm air. Horns blew as tiny cars and trucks raced along the highways' many lanes and ramps, hurrying to each of their destinations.

It reminded Lana of Samuel's matchbox sets, with plastic garages, miniature fuel pumps and tiny rubber tires for those imaginary flats. She thought of how he used to play with his cars for hours, and sometimes, she'd even play too. It was fun; however, it seemed as if one day they both finally outgrew it and the cars and trucks, garage and fuel pumps disappeared into a box in the attic—just like Samuel had disappeared along with her parents.

Suddenly, she began to cry.

Evan spun around and lifted the shield on the welding helmet. "Lana? What's wrong?" He quickly turned off the torch and sat down beside her. "What's the matter? Is it Samuel…or your parents?" Slipping his arms around her, he gently pressed her head against his chest and stroked the back of her hair.

Lana nodded her head and sniffled, trying to slow the tears that ran from her eyes. She knew that if she continued to cry she would begin to transform. So, forcing herself to concentrate on something else, she buried her face within Evan's shirt and focused on the different smells and scents of his clothes and skin.

His skin smelled fresh and invigorating, yet was mixed with the scent of fire and smoke; she figured it was from the welding torch. And, though she made herself listen closely to his soothing words, her tears continued to come.

"Lana, please don't cry. I promise I'll find Samuel for you; if it's the last thing I do. In fact, I was planning on checking on one more thing, then starting out tomorrow morning—alone."

Removing his gloves, he brushed a large teardrop from beneath her eye with his finger. "Please. Besides, you don't wanna make me feel sad on my birthday, do ya?"

She stared up at him with red rimmed eyes and silently shook her head. Her words were choked. "No. We were supposed to do something fun today." A broken smile made an appearance upon her face. "I'm sorry."

"No, no, no. Ssshh." Evan stroked her hair. "You don't ever have to be sorry for missing your brother or your parents. He took her chin in his hand and turned it toward him. "Let me just finish up here and we'll get going." His smile was warm and encouraging. "Besides, your parents would want to see you happy. Don't you agree?"

Lana nodded her head again. "Yeah, you're right," she whispered. "They loved Samuel and me, and *always* wanted to see us happy."

"See, I was right." He stood to his feet. "Now, give

me just a few more minutes and I'll be finished.

Lana wiped her eyes. "Thank you, Evan."

"Thank you for what?"

"For helping me—being there for me." She smiled up at him. "I don't know what I'd do without you."

"Well, I'll do whatever I can to help you. And, if you still wanna go home, that's okay too. But, if anything should happen to me, which it shouldn't; I want you to stay with Ches." The words tugged at his heart as he said them. "He'd help you find Samuel and try to keep you safe. Even though," his words became no more than a whisper, "the thought of you with him makes me sick. And, if he attempted to take you away now, he'd have a fight on his hands."

Replacing his gloves, Evan quickly spun around, pulled the shield down over his face, and went back to work. The air around them was suddenly quiet, nearly awkward and Lana watched him diligently working away, though she was careful not to look at the hot flame or the sparks spurting in every direction.

She wondered what he was thinking.

After a few minutes he was finished. "Welp, that's it. I think they should be happy with it." Sweat beaded his face as he turned to look at her. "Will you be okay while I run the welder down?"

She nodded her head and lightly smiled. "Yeah, I'll just wait here."

"Okay," he said hoisting the heavy piece of machinery onto his back, "I'll be right back." Climbing down was somewhat slow, possibly even slower than his going up, until he reached his webbing,

Lana zoomed in on him, watching his every facial expression—his magnificent grin as he grasped onto his webbing, a scowl and grimace as the welder banged against his back, and his face as he glanced up at her often to make certain she was still okay.

Within a few minutes, he was up the steel structure and by her side. He held tight to her as he helped her to her feet.

"So, are you ready to go?" he asked. His eyes twinkled as the warm breeze blew several strands of dark hair along his face.

Lana slid her arm around his waist and hugged him. "No. Let's just hang out here for a few more minutes. This is great."

The kaleidoscope of colors in his eyes sparkled at her words and his smile appeared. "Yeah, this is great."

Excitedly, Evan pointed out several points on the surrounding countryside, eagerly explaining the various locations and the significance of them. He pointed in the direction of Billet, where the cabins were, and Tarren, where he had first seen her and rescued her from the mob. Bear Mountain was in the far-off distance. He asked her how she had managed to get from there to Tarren.

Lana shrugged. "I don't remember."

"Hmm," Evan scratched his head. "Could be your arachnid had kicked in to its defensive mode and pushed you to survival. You don't remember anything?"

"Well, I was wrapped in my cocoon and remember seeing Samuel leave for help. Then, I guess I passed out. And, when I awoke, my webbing was gone and I tried to find my way out of the woods. I ate a few berries along the way—stuff my father had taught us was okay to eat; but, I was so hungry and tired by the time I got to town, I ended up right in front of the bakeshop..." She paused. "Well, you know the rest. I don't know what I would've done if you hadn't come along."

"Ches and Trey would have helped you," he added sourly.

"Yeah, I guess," she replied. "But, I don't know..." her words trailed off.

"Well..." he was suddenly serious, "...there's one last thing I wanna show you before we leave."

"Brant Military Base, the military base that you and Samuel were taken to, is to the North." He pointed in that direction. "Now, from what I've been able to find out, Samuel was taken back there..."

"What?" Lana's hands flew to her chest then quickly to Evan's arm for support. "You know he's there?"

"I'm certain of it." Sighing heavily, he scowled. "Though, the place is loaded with security and it's gonna' be difficult to get him out."

He glanced down at her. "I didn't tell you, but they had me there. It was several years ago and there was a Doctor there by the name of Vaun Page—the sick bastard—and that crazy young assistant of his, Doctor Horn. I think she had just graduated from Nazi school or something. What a bit…"

"Doctor Horn? Did you say Doctor Horn? I think I remember her. She was the one who came to see me and Samuel. "

"Yeah," he remarked bitterly. The name was like acid on his tongue. "If I'da had any sense I would've killed those two."

"How did they find you and how long were you there?"

"Six years—six long years I was there, until an acquaintance of mine was able to get me out. They had caught me because I was sloppy. I knew that there were others like me, others who could relate to what I was and what I was going through, maybe even have a cure. I could sense them through my arachnid beast. And, one, I'm certain, was close to the cabin—possibly within a couple of miles.

Then, suddenly one day, their scent just disappeared. I believe that it was a ploy, a plan to catch any of the black widows that still existed."

"So, they know that there are other black widows out there?" Lana's mouth dropped open.

"Sure, they do. They're the ones responsible for all this mess. They were dumping toxic crap into the waters up in the mountains and it infected all the plant and animal life in the area."

"Hey, I caught some blue tadpoles up there for my

fish tank."

"Yep," he nodded his head. "More than likely they were infected."

"Well, they didn't seem hostile or anything; they were just blue," she responded.

"Well, from what I overheard from a few of the soldiers at the military base, different things had different reactions to the chemicals. And, they weren't just any chemicals; they were bio-warfare chemicals.

The fish and aqua life became larger, more colorful, and were unsafe for anyone to eat, plus most of the animal life in the area died; however, the black widow spider thrived and became more aggressive. In fact, they became *very* aggressive. And, although there was supposed to have been several people who were bitten, I never saw a one—only sensed them.

I was kept by myself; and, they did every damn experiment on me they could. I thought I would go insane, and may have, if it hadn't been for all the medication they kept givin' me."

Suddenly, Evan noticed Lana staring at him in horror. He had said too much.

"Oh geeze, I'm sorry." He smacked the palm of his hand to the side of his head. "That was a long time ago. I'm sure it's different now."

Lana's hands were trembling as she gently touched his arm. "Please, Evan, we have to get Samuel outta there."

He stared into her frightened eyes. "We will. I

promise. So, let's get going now. I wanna' stop and pick up my pay then head out just beyond Bridgeton. I have a few questions for someone who lives out that way."

"Okay." She meekly nodded her head as she stared off in the distance wondering where her little brother might be.

Chapter 17

Evan watched the macadam rushing toward him as he steered the motorcycle in the direction of the next county and Jacob Winslow. His earlier discussion with Lana had caused many of the horrible, repressed memories of his time spent at the military facility to surface. They ran through the nerves beneath his skin and his mind like an old horror movie projector which continued to click through one scene—a bloody scene.

The old voices scratched at his brain; and, he could hear each person as if they were a passenger on the back of his bike whispering their deep-seeded evil intentions into his ear.

It was the sound of the different guards' voices and the scads of assistants ready to do whatever it took to achieve results and get answers. Doctor Lanette Horn's young, however snappish commands, were cold and callous, a voice from the tomb. And, Doctor Vaun Page, a German scientist straight from the holocaust spoke very seldom. However, when he did, his German accent, so thick and garbled, was only understood by those possessing the same warped mind as he, or those who were about to be experimented on.

Evan's ability to transform into a black widow, compounded with his ability to retain youth, made *him* the primary subject.

Angrily, he fought the horrible memories that now flooded his mind, the voices that rose above the hum of the motorcycle's motor and the passing of other automobiles. However, they continued to come.

"Doctor Vaun Page," he could hear Doctor Horn's younger, stone cold voice saying, "we have patient number 01131—Evan Labonte—ready for you sir. Would you like for us to medicate him before you start?"

Evan could hear Doctor Vaun Page clearing his throat, the snapping of his rubber gloves as he slid them on, and the flicking of his middle finger against the glass syringe. Sniffing twice, he finally answered. "A minimal amount, to impede full mutation. I want to see if the webbing will produce on its own as a defense mechanism for the human body. Is the guard in place?"

"Yes, Doctor—armed and ready."

"Good," he replied in a thick garble. "Then, let us begin."

"What are you planning on doing?" Evan screamed. His body shook and his head pounded from the medication as he yanked at the restraints pinning him face down on the table.

"You may feel a slight prick," Doctor Vaun Page answered. "Just hold still."

"You, hold still!" Evan shouted. "And, let me stick you!"

Vaun Page pushed his thick black-framed glasses

back on his nose. Perspiration lightly misted his forehead; he smelled of after-shave.

"Miss Horn, kindly have the subject gagged."

"Yes, Doctor." She readily motioned to the guard and he promptly appeared with a cloth gag in hand. "Bind his mouth officer," she requested as she stepped to the side.

"Yes, ma'am." The guard's hands moved quickly, efficiently, as Evan struggled and shook his head. "Knock it off." His elbow met with the back of Evan's skull and a lightning bolt of pain rushed through Evan's face as his forehead hit the steel table and the dampness raced to his eyes.

"Ugh!" His muffled cry was caught by the wad of material covering his mouth and his eyes flashed to black as he glared back at the soldier.

"All right, lieutenant. That's enough," Doctor Horn remarked. "We need accurate results, not results from your brashness."

"Sorry, Doctor Horn—my apologies." Quickly, he backed away from the table. "Will you be needing me for anything else?"

"Just remain close," she retorted.

Nodding his head, he immediately retreated and stood by the laboratory door.

Doctor Vaun Page slowly ran his thick fingers along the crimson streaks imbedded on both sides of Evan's lower back; then, he cleared his gravelly throat.

"Doctor Horn, make note of the eight markings

on the abdomen, posterior view—size, form, etc. Then, after the injection, I want a full report on subject of any modifications—elevation in body temperature, pupil discoloration, which is already apparent," he said as he glanced into Evan's steely eyes, "and, any other mutations or changes."

"Yes, sir."

"Well, let us see if we can figure out how that webbing of yours is produced." He raised his glasses and quickly glanced at Evan's chart, "Subject 01131." Flicking the syringe for a second time, he quickly and accurately jabbed it into one of the red streaks along Evan's back.

"Ugh!" Evan jumped as the long broad needle was stuck beneath his skin and the burning liquid entered his body. The doctor then pushed to bury the four inches of steel into his back.

"Goddd!" Evan cried into the gag as he pressed his hips to the table. Sweat beads popped upon his face and he gasped for breath.

"Hmm." The doctor watched as the red streak began to pucker and the miniscule-sized pores split. Quickly, he grabbed the over-head light and the immense magnifying lens and positioned them closer to the marking.

"An extraction, doctor," the garbled command rose from Vaun Page's scratchy throat.

Doctor Horn immediately spun and grabbed another syringe off a nearby tray.

“Hold this one.” He hurriedly took a specially designed three-pronged syringe from her and stuck it into the same red streak along Evan’s back.

Evan groaned and dug his fingers into the cold of the operating table as webbing began to pour from the engorging streak.

Vaun Page worked fervently to gather tissue sample as the silky strands steadily grew in length. Quickly applying pressure, he pushed the three pronged extractor deeper into Evan’s skin.

Sweat burst upon Evan’s body from head to foot as he fought to catch his breath; and, suddenly arching his back, his body slammed against the table.

The three-pronged extractor ripped from his skin and crashed to the floor, while Doctor Horn fought with both hands to retain control of her syringe.

“Gah!” Doctor Vaun Page’s caterpillar brows came together in an angry knot and his curses were vehement, deep-rooted German growls.

“Lieutenant!” he snarled. “Restrain the subject!” The guard immediately came to assistance. And, pulling the additional straps from beneath the table, he rapidly fastened them across Evan’s body, yanked them tight and secured the latches.

“He should be good now,” he remarked.

“Good,” Doctor Vaun Page gruffly stated as he repositioned his glasses and readily grabbed another extractor. “Miss Horn, is the syringe still imbedded beneath the skin?”

"Yes, Doctor. I was able to just barely hang on."

"Good," he replied. "Now—let us begin again."

Evan shook his head and pulled the motorcycle to the side of the road. He was trembling.

"Evan? What's wrong?" Lana leaned forward and spoke softly into his ear. "Are you okay? You're shaking."

Glancing into the rearview mirror, he blinked his eyes. They were black as coal and his appearance was beginning to slightly change—not from the wind which blew through his dark hair or upon his face, it was the angered creature inside him wanting to come alive.

He shook his head again. "It's nothing." And, pressing the gear shifter into first, he pulled back out onto the road.

They traveled south, along the windy stretch of road leading away from Tarren. And, after covering several miles of desolate, mountainous roads, they came to a sharp bend. Evan downshifted and turned right.

"We're here," he stated as he slowed the bike to avoid the several pot-holes that were gouged deep within the dirt road. The various rows of trees surrounding them broke as they arrived at a small clearing where numerous flowers covered the entire lawn of a lovely little cottage.

A miniature flat-faced dog waddled its way across the front porch and down the steps. And, lazily trotting over to Lana and Evan, it bellowed out a friendly welcome. Lana stared down at it as Evan happily patted its head and chuckled.

"Hey Maggie, haven't seen you in a long time." Maggie gleefully licked Evan's hand and wagged her tail. Then, she attempted to reach for Lana with her long slobbering tongue. Lana immediately drew her hand away.

"Oh, its okay. She won't bite." Evan took her hand and helped her from the bike. Then, he climbed off and stretched. Maggie jumped up to lick him again; however, the short stubbles she had for legs, buckled beneath her weight and she clumsily toppled backward to the ground. Evan laughed aloud as Lana hid a giggle behind her hand.

"Maggie! Maggie!" Two young, scarlet-haired children, barefoot and in bathing suits, ran around the corner of the house and shouted.

One was a young boy and the other looked to be his twin; however, she was female and slightly smaller. Dark goggles were strapped around the boy's head and a snorkel hose stood tall, waving salutations from his head. And, despite the large pink tube around her small waist, the young girl kept time with her brother. Water dripped from their hair and clothing as they both stopped short in front of Evan and Lana.

"Uncle!" They both announced gleefully as large smiles crested their faces.

"Check out my new snorkel!" The boy excitedly blew on the mouthpiece and water spurted from the top. His twin sister leapt forward and eagerly tried to wrap her arms and the huge tube around Evan's waist. Evan gently patted the back of her wet hair and kissed her on the crown of her head. Lana watched out of curiosity.

"Hey guys! How are you?" He reached into his pocket, past the wad of cash he received for the job he had done at the construction site, and pulled out two red hot fireballs.

"Now, keep these in your mouths and out of the carpet. Your mom wasn't too happy when you put the gum I gave you in your sister's hair, Aimery. And, Aimee, if that fireball gets too hot, just spit it in the trash can, no givin' it to Maggie. She'll end up with her butt on fire in more ways than one."

Aimery and Aimee laughed.

"Yeah," Aimee giggled, "her butt was nearly on fire this morning when Daddy caught her in the trash. She's a little piggy!"

"Yeah, she is!" Aimery added while imitating a pig, "*Oink! Oink!*"

They all laughed, then started toward the house.

"Aw, poor Maggie," Evan patted her head again.

"Is everyone making fun of you?"

Aimery and Aimee ran ahead and called out in unison, "Momma, Momma, Uncle Evan's here!"

Lana glanced over at him out of the corner of her eye; her one brow was arched to her hair. "Uncle?"

Evan smiled sheepishly. "They call me *Uncle* because I've known their father so long; they think Jacob and I are brothers.

Lana tilted her head in confusion. "I don't think I understand."

"Jacob Winslow knew Grandmother Hobbs. He's the one who helped me escape the military compound."

"Now, I'm really confused." Lana stopped in her tracks. "Jacob Winslow knew Grandmother Hobbs, who has been gone for years now; so, that means he has to be ancient. Yet, you say, his *small* children think that *you* and *he* are brothers? And, from what you were saying earlier, you were also at the compound with Doctor Horn who was with me and Samuel. None of it makes any sense. There's too many years difference."

"Let me elaborate a little." Evan scratched the back of his neck. "Jacob knew Grandmother because they worked together at another facility studying the effects the chemicals, they were using as weapons, had on the plant and animal life. He and Grandmother worked in the lab and confided with one another on everything—things they didn't even share with their own families. Now, I know Doctor Horn because of my idiocy of eight years ago when I was caught. And, I know Jacob Winslow because he took and used some of *my* blood on himself…"

Chapter 18

Lana had been so engrossed in Evan's explanation that she hadn't even heard the front door to the cottage open. A young woman stepped out onto the porch. Lana stared at her emerald green eyes that danced with every movement she made and long flowing, auburn hair that was fashioned back in a black-velvet bow. Her attire was simple, white top and long pleated black skirt. She was absolutely lovely.

Aimery and Aimee, who were chatting exuberantly, led her by the arms, down the steps and across the yard.

Rolling her eyes, she allowed them to lead her over to where Lana and Evan stood.

"Evan," she immediately embraced him. "It's been so long since we've seen you." A broad smile accompanied the warm twinkle in her eyes. "Does Jacob know you're here?"

"I don't think so; not unless the Winslow welcoming committee," he smiled at the children, "notified him."

Lucinda looked upon the children with an abundance of love, while Aimery and Aimee were now walking alongside her, each holding her hand. They were quiet as church mice except for the irking squeak of Aimee's rubber floatie and the occasion gurgle of air that burst through Aimery's snorkel as he breathed in time with his steps. "They certainly are something, aren't they?" she remarked.

"Yeah, I'd say," Evan grinned at them.

"So, Evan..." The woman turned to look at Lana and winked, "you haven't introduced me to your friend."

"Oh, I'm sorry. This is Lana, Lana Patterson." He then turned to Lana. "Lana, this is Lucinda Winslow."

Lucinda smiled. "It's my pleasure to meet you, Lana. Welcome to our home."

"Thank you," Lana replied, as they again began to walk toward the house. "You have such a lovely home. The flowers are absolutely beautiful."

"Thank you," she replied. "It doesn't seem that anyone else around here appreciates them as much as I do."

"I do, Mama!" Aimee chimed in. "I love your flowers."

"Well, thank you, honey," her mother responded. "Now, why don't you two run along and let your father know that Uncle Evan is here to see him, and that lunch is ready." Her hand slipped from theirs and they hurriedly raced across the yard, around the corner of the house and out of sight.

Maggie plopped down in the grass at Lucinda's feet, deciding it was less work not to follow them. "Let's go into the house; I just finished making lunch. Are you hungry?"

Lana and Evan nodded their heads.

"Good. Then, it's settled; you'll eat with us. I made tuna salad sandwiches, a fruit salad and a homemade peach pie. It's still in the oven, but it should be finished soon."

"That sounds great, Lucinda." Evan grinned. "We really appreciate it."

"Yes," Lana added. "Thank you."

"It's my pleasure, sweetie." She patted Lana's hand. "Now, come on in and get washed up."

The front door opened and the scent of warm peaches flooded their noses. It was tantalizing, teasing, could be tasted upon their tongues. Lana's mouth began to water and her stomach rumbled. Evan glanced over at her and smiled.

The cottage was just as lovely inside as out. It looked like one of those pictured in a woman's home catalog and made Lana think of home.

In a few steps, they were by-passing the living room and heading toward the kitchen.

"The restroom's just inside that door." Lucinda pointed to a door that was just off the kitchen. "You can wash your hands then take a seat." She quickly grabbed a pot holder and opened the oven door to check the pie.

Suddenly, the back door burst open and Aimee and Aimery entered.

"Oh no, you two—snorkel and tube outside on the deck." Her voice was stern, yet gentle and sweet.

"Aw, Momma!"

"Listen to your mother, you two," a male's voice sounded behind them.

Lana had just stepped out of the bathroom to see Jacob Winslow walking in, and she immediately paused at the sight of him.

He was tall, seemingly aged in demeanor, yet young in appearance. He had the same dark hair and features that Evan had, yet they were slightly more accentuated, somewhat shadowed. Regardless, he was very handsome and seemed almost regal in manner.

Lana found herself staring. His black eyes swiftly shot from Evan to her and the kitchen became unbearably quiet.

"Are you okay, dear?" Lucinda asked Lana.

Her soft voice broke through Lana's candid fixation and the discomforting quiet. Blushing, Lana blinked her eyes.

"Oh, I'm sorry," she stammered as she awkwardly found a seat next to Evan at the table.

Smiling warmly, Lucinda replied, "No need to be sorry my dear; this is my husband, Jacob. He tends to get that reaction from everyone who first meets him." She placed a plate of food before her and Evan. "You must be hungry, now, eat up."

Jacob quietly stepped behind Lucinda and lovingly wrapped his arms around her waist. Lucinda turned her face toward him and he gently placed a kiss on her cheek.

“Everything looks delicious, dear.”

“Thank you,” she responded. “I hope you’re hungry.”

“Famished,” he stated as he stepped away from her and placed a hand on his stomach. He then glanced at the children. “Aimery and Aimee, you two may say grace.”

Quickly, the twins bolted upright in their seats, placed their hands together and began to pray in unison. “Thank you, God, for this food; and, thank you for our mom and dad.” Briefly, their eyes locked then closed. “And, thank you for Uncle Evan and Auntie Lana.” Giggling, they opened their eyes. “Amen!”

Lucinda smiled at the twins and then at Jacob. “That was lovely. Now, let’s eat.”

Lana was too hungry to notice how quickly anyone else was eating; though, when she finished first, she glanced shamefacedly around the table at the others who were still working on the first half of their cut sandwiches.

“Auntie Lana is hungry!” Aimery and Aimee chimed together as they began to giggle. Quickly imitating her, they wolfed down their sandwiches.

“Now, children, that isn’t very nice,” Lucinda mildly scolded them as she reached across the table and patted Lana’s hand. “It’s okay, dear; if you’re hungry, you go ahead and eat. There’s plenty where that came from. Would you like another sandwich?” Her warming smile was reassuring, motherly, and Lana immediately knew she liked Lucinda. And, though she still had fruit salad sitting before her in a small dessert cup and warm peach pie coming, she couldn't resist.

"May I?"

"Of course you may." Lucinda stated as she pushed her chair back and retrieved another sandwich off a serving platter holding several.

The twins began to giggle and Jacob shot them a warning glance from the corner of his coal black eyes; then, his gaze settled on Lana and he momentarily watched her.

"So, what brings you out here, Evan?" His gaze left her and he and Evan's eyes met.

Evan's prismatic eyes swirled with an array of colors: blues and golds, browns, yellows and greens; while, Jacob's remained an inky black and void of all emotion.

Evan watched, with the ability of his highly developed vision, both Jacob and Lucinda, as Lucinda placed another sandwich on his and Lana's plate. Then, he spoke.

"Lana's been turned."

"I know," Jacob replied. "I knew the minute you two were within a five mile radius of here. Her scent as a female is strong."

Lana blushed and quickly took a bite of her sandwich, pretending they were discussing something like motors or fishing, anything but her.

"Well, she was at "Brant" and her parents helped her get away."

“Where are her parents now?” Jacob waved his wife away as she approached his plate with another sandwich. Then, he motioned for her to take the children outside.

“*Aw, but, Momma,* we wanna’ stay and watch Auntie Lana eat some more.”

“Sshhh, children. Your father has important business to discuss with Uncle Evan, so let’s walk down to the garden and check on mother’s pears.”

“*Oh, okay,*” they sung in unison. Then, within moments, they were running across the yard and disappearing into the woods.

Jacob watched as his wife vanished into the trees behind them, then his dark stare returned to Evan. “Now, you were saying that she was in Brant and her parents helped her get away. And, the question I asked was: Where are her parents now?”

Evan grabbed Lana’s hand beneath the table. “They were killed trying to get her out.”

Jacob’s eyes cut to Lana. “I’m sorry for your loss. But, that still doesn’t explain why you’re here.”

“Well, there’s also a matter of a younger brother who was also bitten, held at Brant, then escaped. Now, the problem is, we don’t know where he is. However, from some of the information I was able to gather, I think he’s back at Brant and being held there.”

Jacob sat back in his chair and eyed Evan suspiciously. “So, what does all this have to do with me?”

"I may need your help getting him out."

"And, what makes you think I would jeopardize everything I have here to help you?"

"Well…" Evan sat forward; his countless years of existence bringing about an uncanny, almost ennoble, authority. "Because, *you* know the layout; and, *you* can get him out of there."

Jacob's black irises sizzled beneath his lids as his eyes slowly crept to Lana. A round moment passed and then he spoke. "Lucinda is with child again; and I won't have the same reoccurrence as last time."

Lana's gaze shot to Evan.

"It won't," Evan replied.

"And, what certainty do you have of this?"

Evan's tone was marked. "There are no certainties in life, Jacob. You know that as well as I. It is what it is." Evan slid his chair back from the table and stood. "Look, I'll give you three days to decide; then, I'll go it alone."

"Come on, Lana." Evan quickly took her hand then turned back to Jacob. "Tell Lucinda and the twins 'goodbye' for me, and thank Lucinda for the delicious lunch."

Evan led Lana from the kitchen and toward the living room. They walked in silence from the house, down the cottage steps, and across the yard.

Lucinda suddenly called to them from the porch.

"Evan…Lana…hold on a minute." She smiled thoughtfully and held up a small bundle she had in her hand. “You forgot your pie.” Winking, she made her way toward them; then, she took both of Lana’s hands and placed the small bundle in them. It was warm to the touch and the scent of peaches was heavenly. Lana couldn’t conceal the gratitude that appeared in her beaming grin.

“I wrapped it for you in a kerchief since you’re on the bike. I hope you enjoy it.” She hugged Lana. “Come back and see us again, dear. And, don’t let Jacob frighten you off; he’s just a little temperamental some days, but the majority of the time he’s as gentle as a lamb.” Then, she stepped in front of Evan and took his face in both her hands; her emerald eyes locked on his. “And, don’t you let him say no to you. I’ll talk to him this evening and have him give you a call by tomorrow night. He just needs some time to think.”

“Thank you for everything, Lucinda.” He gave her a hug, being careful not to press against her stomach. They remained that way for a brief moment. Then, Evan pulled away and stated, “Oh, and congratulations on the new baby.”

Gently, he placed his hand on the tiny bulge of her belly and smiled. “Maybe this one will have dark hair and look like Jacob.”

“Yes, we hope so. Three red-heads in the family are quite enough.”

The twins suddenly burst through the front door, jumped from the porch and raced across the yard.

Their hair was dry now and their scarlet locks shone like licking flames in the afternoon sun.

Chapter 19

Lana and Evan rode in silence for several miles as Lana's head lay against Evan's back and his shirt swirled with the wind about her face. She could hear him breathing and the ratta-tat-tat of his beating heart; however, the words of Jacob Winslow and his wife still rang loudly within her ears.

"Evan," she spoke into his ear. The wind swept the tips of his dark locks along her nose; it tickled. "I need to know what's going on. What's going on between you and Jacob Winslow?"

"I'll have to explain later," he responded over his shoulder.

"No. Can you please tell me now? Please. I need to know."

Evan sighed then downshifted and leaned, guiding the bike to the shoulder a safe distance off the road. Parking, he turned it off. Then, he twisted around in his seat to look at her. His eyes were a flurry of animated colors.

"Jacob Winslow and I have a difficult time seeing eye-to-eye," he began. "It started years ago when he and Grandmother Hobbs had begun working together after the military realized the seriousness of their foul up in dumping their so-called *nuclear waste.*

See, the whole area was considered *active* with

radiation and the work he and Grandmother did became top-secret—priority. Even their families weren't allowed to know what they were working on or what they were doing.

Well, when Grandmother Hobbs discovered me and found out that I had been infected, she and Jacob's curiosity and studies intensified. Grandmother was more interested in finding a cure for me; however, Jacob was more interested in the longevity of life that came with the mutation.

So, against Grandmother's wishes and unknown to the military, he decided to inject himself with a sample of my blood, use himself as a human guinea pig."

Evan paused and glanced around at their surroundings; then, he reached up and ran a hand along his mussed hair. "How do I explain this?" He turned his attention back to Lana.

"Well, the military found out about Jacob's little secret and decided to hold him; and, they began studies on him and I. That's when Doctor Vaun Page…" The name brought a sour taste to his mouth. "…was brought onboard. And, when they found out that Jacob, in the meantime, had a girlfriend that he had impregnated, Lucinda…"

"Well, wouldn't that mean that she had received some of his blood through…?" Her voice trailed off.

"Yeah." Evan nodded his head. "Though, she had no idea of what Jacob was doing or what he was involved in."

"Oh, my gosh! So, Lucinda is one of us." Lana's mouth hung to her chin as she quietly repeated Lucinda's name. Then, her eyes bolted open at the thought of the twin's role in all this.

"And, the twins?" She quickly searched Evan's face.

"The twins are different. But, let me backup a little and explain about Lucinda first. See, Lucinda can transform because of receiving Jacob's blood through his se…"

Lana's hand quickly shot in the air. "I think we can skip that part. I think we both understand."

Evan's brows arched and a boyish smile surfaced on his lips. "Anyway, Lucinda can transform; however, each time she reverted back to her human self, she aged."

"She aged?"

"Yeah—by several years too. See, when she and Jacob had gotten together, she was quite young, about your age. And, he was about the age he looks now, maybe twenty-four, twenty-five. However, now, she looks like she's about thirty. Somehow, the process works differently on her." He paused.

"Would you like to stand and stretch a little before I go on?" He had noticed Lana squirming.

Nodding her head, Lana placed a hand on his shoulder, balanced herself and got off. Then, Evan hopped off also.

Each took their turn at bending and twisting, then

Evan took her hand. "Come on, let's go for a walk."

"But, what about the bike? Will it be okay?"

"Yeah, I can sense if anyone comes within a few hundred yards of it. You should be able to also." Lana just nodded her head.

"Now, back to Lucinda. When the military found out about Jacob's own little testing, they immediately investigated all and every faction of his life; and, as soon as they found out that he had impregnated Lucinda, they nabbed her and took her to the lab. Jacob was there when they brought her in; and, they tried to reassure him that it was the best thing for her and the baby, which they soon found out were *babies*.

Anyway, Vaun Page had other ideas for Lucinda besides baby showers and prenatal care. See, something was different about the twins. They were growing at an insurmountable rate, the rate of a normal black widow egg's incubation period. Lucinda was only pregnant for twenty-eight days."

Lana stopped in her tracks. "Twenty-eight days! She was only pregnant for twenty-eight days with twins!"

Evan nodded his head. "Yeah; and the entire time Jacob was a mess. See, they had them in the lab together so they could monitor Jacob's arachnid responses to Lucinda and her babies. Well, when Vaun Page and anyone else tried to touch Lucinda, Jacob nearly went insane. See, Lucinda was *his* arachnid female; and, if there was any other male around her, even human,

Jacob went nuts."

Lana interrupted again. "*Oh*, so that explains the tension between *you two*—because of Lucinda." They continued to walk.

"Right," Evan stated. "But now, also, because of you." He stopped and turned toward her. "See, male arachnids will kill each other in the blink of an eye over a female black widow. It's just the nature of their species. Heck, that's the way it is with a lot of species—they're very protective of their females or their mates. Anyway, that's why some males have a very difficult time getting along."

"Like you and Ches," Lana added.

He frowned. "Yeah, like me and Ches."

A tingling sensation ran along Lana's spine at the thought of Evan thinking of her as his mate—*his* arachnid female. She smiled to herself; then, she quietly turned to him and asked, "So, do you think of *me* as your arachnid female?"

The various-colored gems in his eyes sparkled to life, as flush rushed to his cheeks and he thought for a moment. "Yes. Yes, I do." His index finger traced her cheek. "I don't wanna' share you with anyone."

"Well, you won't have to." She gently placed a kiss on his cheek. "Because, I don't wanna' share you with anyone either."

Evan teased, "Not even Diana?"

"Especially not her!" Lana pinched him on the arm and he laughed.

“She sure is something else, isn’t she,” he stated.

Lana’s eyes narrowed. “I guess.”

“Well, she’s been a good friend to me. In fact, the only friend I’ve had.”

Lana scowled. “Well, I think she wants to be more than just friends.”

Evan lightly laughed. “I guess so. But, don’t you ever worry about that.” Pulling her toward him, he hugged her tightly.

A moment passed; then, he released her. His eyes were bright and a crooked smile was on his face. “Now, do you wanna’ hear the rest of the story?”

“Yeah.” She took his hand as they turned around and headed back in the direction of the motorcycle.

“Well, as I was saying, Jacob became crazy, nearly insane, especially when Vaun Page started poking around Lucinda wanting to do tests on the unborn fetuses. Lucinda became so despondent that she couldn’t eat or sleep. She was so upset with Jacob and upset with the doctors; it nearly caused her to miscarry.”

The toe of Evan’s boot dug at the stones lining the edge of the road. Then, he continued.

“Anyway, Lucinda’s condition worsened and the good doctor…” Evan made quotation marks with his fingers, “…and his so-called trusty subordinates rushed in to revive her and the unborn babies. Well, Jacob went absolutely ballistic. And, though he was medicated, he transformed and broke free from his bonds, tore through the compound and killed several guards before getting Lucinda outta' there."

Evan stopped and turned to Lana. He watched her wide eyes as they stared into the empty space before them, most likely visualizing the same thing he was. However, he knew it had been worse than anything she could ever imagine.

From what Evan had heard, Jacob had not only killed the guards, but had also ripped them to shreds and consumed several body parts as he rampaged through the military base leaving behind a wave of carnage.

Lana softly spoke. "So, that explains what he meant by, "not allowing a reoccurrence. He's afraid that if he gets involved, Lucinda and the twins will be in danger."

Evan nodded his head. "Exactly. Right now, they live quiet, secluded lives, away from the outside world; and, if Jacob had his way, he would never socialize with anyone.

However, when they escaped, Jacob was still in his arachnid form, unaware of the harm he was doing to Lucinda and the twins as he made his way out of the complex and away to safety.

When, he finally transformed back into his human state, Lucinda was in critical condition and the unborn babies were in severe distress. Fortunate for them, Jacob had stored several vials of my blood at a hidden location where he had taken them."

"What? He kept your blood?"

Evan's features darkened as he silently nodded. "Yes, he kept my blood—*without* my permission.

Anyway, he injected Lucinda with it and she ended up immediately going into labor. She had only been pregnant for several weeks, but the babies were full term and ready to be delivered.

"Gee," Lana breathed.

"Well, I won't go into the gory details of the delivery; but, I heard it was bad. See, now that Lucinda was directly injected with my blood, her body insisted on transforming to arachnid form, but regardless of the severe pain she was going through, she probably would have killed the twins, possibly even eaten them."

"Eww, that's terrible." Lana's features fought between sadness and disgust.

"Yeah," Evan agreed. "Meeting her, you wouldn't think she could hurt a fly."

"I know," Lana stated. "She seems like the nicest person ever. All of that must've been hard on her."

Evan quietly nodded. "It took years for Lucinda to come to grips with everything and forgive Jacob for what he had done."

"But, don't the children have to go to school and that?" Lana asked, "And, can *they* transform?"

"Well, to answer your first question, they're basically off the grid with how they live. However, Jacob and Lucinda would never allow Aimery and Aimee to grow up to be illiterate; so, Lucinda home schools. And, as a result, the two are very bright.

And, to answer your second question, they're still not sure. The children have never displayed any type of arachnid behavior other than aging at an abnormal rate. They may look like they're ten, but in all actuality they're close to my age."

"They're *your* age?"

Evan grinned as he rocked on his heels. "Yeah. And, it all seems kinda' funny."

Lana turned and looked at him. "What does?"

A slight hue had colored his cheeks. "Well, I always wondered what my children would be like, especially when I'm around those two rascals."

Lana blushed and began to walk toward the motorcycle which sat just ahead. Then, she whispered, "I'd imagine they'd be cute as buttons."

"Whadja' say?" Evan asked as he caught up to her and turned her toward him.

"Oh, nothing. I was just wondering where we're headed to now. It is your birthday you know. We have to do something special today."

Evan looked into her eyes and gently touched her nose. "Cute as buttons, huh?"

It was Lana's turn to blush. "You weren't supposed to hear that."

Evan smiled and softly laughed. "You'd be surprised what I hear."

"Like what?"

"Oh, nothing." Releasing her hand, he walked

toward the bike.

"Hey, I wanna' know what you hear."

"Oh, just those little puffing sounds you make at night." His eyes sparkled wickedly and he laughed.

"Hey! That's not fair. You've been listening to me when I sleep."

Evan reached the motorcycle and Lana caught up to him. Then, she playfully shoved him.

"But, it's so cute," he commented as he grabbed her around the waist and pulled her toward him. His eyes met hers and locked. "I listen to it every night."

Lana began to protest, however, Evan's lips found hers and drown out her words. Then, pulling away, he climbed onto the bike and patted the seat behind him for her to climb on.

Chapter 20

The onyx-colored motorcycle cut into each curve of the road, straightened, then cut again. Its speed was incredible and the mountainous road and surrounding trees rushed by them in a rich, green and brown, blur.

They raced in the direction of Aune' and the carnival that had been there for the entire week. This was to be the last day and Evan had decided that he and Lana both needed a bit of R and R before he was to venture into Bear Mountain territory, and Brant Military Base, in search of Samuel. If Samuel was being held captive there, it would be tough, but, he was determined to bring him out.

Dedication to Lana's happiness had become his main concern; and, bringing her and her brother together was key. He wasn't sure if it was the arachnid beast within him that desired to please her in any way he could; or, if it was just his deep-inept feelings for her that made him want to see her happy. Either way, he didn't care.

Evan spoke over his shoulder to her. "We won't stay long, just long enough to grab something to eat and check out a few of the stands if you like. Then, you need to go shopping."

"It's okay. We can stay as long as you like," she answered between the locks of his wafting hair and into his ear.

Evan slowed the bike and pulled into a parking spot just outside the entrance of the carnival. Shutting it off, he helped Lana to her feet then climbed off. Smiling, he reached for her hand.

"I guess you could consider this our first date." He glanced out the corner of his eye to check her reaction.

"I guess," she replied. "This is the first date I've *ever* been on." Lana looked at him in hopes of hearing the same. "Is it yours?"

"Well, no," he gently answered. "You have to remember, I am over 100 years old."

Lana's shoulders tensed at the thought, while a slight twinge of pain raced to her heart. "I know one of them was probably with Diana."

"Well, yeah," Evan answered. "But, that was different. She would occasionally invite me to something and I would go."

Lana paused, nearly stopping in your footsteps. "Were there other girls?"

Evan stopped and looked at her. "Do you really wanna' know about this?"

Lana blushed. "Well, yes and no. It just bothers me; that's all."

His lips brushed along her forehead. "Don't let it. You're the only one for me and the past is what it is."

"Yeah, but, it doesn't mean I have to like it."

"You're right. It's the same for me. I didn't like you

being around Ches." Evan's arms wrapped snuggly around her and he pulled her to his chest. "Now, come on. Let's not talk about this right now; let's go have some fun."

"Yeah," she reluctantly replied. "You're right. We probably have the rest of eternity to talk about it."

Evan's perfect smile was warm and his kaleidoscopic eyes twinkled. "I think I like the sound of that."

The sun's unrelenting rays had barely lessened as Evan and Lana made their way inside to a multicolored booth, paid the attendant and had their hands stamped. The man, seasoned in years and sitting on a stool behind the hazy glass, shifted in his seat then smiled. "Carnival closes at midnight. Enjoy yourselves."

Evan nodded as he slipped the change from the twenty dollar bill he had given the man into his pocket. "Thank you, sir." Then, he took Lana's hand and led her in through the heavy iron gates.

The carnival was set up on several acres of land just outside the town of Aune'. The atmosphere was filled with the sounds of children giggling, rides going, balloons popping, and an attendant shouting out numbers for bingo. The delicious scents of cotton candy, funnel cake and Italian sausage filled the air.

Lana breathed deep, eagerly taking in the smell of each and every item that was being served or cooked. She was amazed at the numerous amounts of scents she could pick up and distinguish. And, though she had eaten earlier, and they still had the peach pie secured in a bag on the back of the motorcycle, her appetite soared and she stared in the direction of a small stand serving ice cream over warm waffles.

"Would you like one?" Evan asked her.

"Definitely!" she grinned.

Excitedly, approaching the stand, they quickly ordered two, gobbled them down and headed in the direction of another food stand. At this one, they ordered French fries, cheeseburgers, a vanilla shake and a chocolate shake. These disappeared quickly, also.

Evan stood rubbing his stomach. "Boy, if we keep this up, we'll have to call a truck out to haul us home." He glanced over at Lana and she stuck her tongue out at him.

Numerous rides were going and the sounds of the metal car racing along the roller coaster tracks and screeching to a halt echoed loudly in Lana's ears. Briefly, she concentrated to reduce the various noises that would end up screaming throughout her head and give her a major migraine. This would take some getting use to.

Evan watched her. "Is it the noise?" he asked.

"Yeah. I just have'ta get used to tuning different things out."

"Yeah, that's how it was with me at first. Even a flies wings flapping was annoying. It sounded like a propeller on a plane."

Lana frowned. “I guess life will be completely different from now on.”

Evan put his arm around her. His voice was comforting. “Well, we’ll try to make it as normal as possible. So, come on, let’s get on a ride or play something, whatever you wanna do.”

Lana’s first choice was the enormous, candy-décor merry-go-round. It was decorated magnificently with colorful, over-sized gumdrops, bubble-gum balls, and various sparkling horses whose necks were laced with wreaths of tootsie rolls.

Evan smiled and teasingly stated, “Still thinking about food, huh?”

Lana playfully elbowed him and led him in the direction of the booth to purchase tickets for the ride.

They rode several things after that, giggling and chatting amongst themselves, though Lana was aware of the long glances of both the young *and* older females, which crossed Evan’s path. They couldn’t help but stare.

He looked young and vibrant with his dark wavy hair and warm velvety eyes. Also, he appeared somehow regal, assured of himself, like he had experienced the whole world in the eighteen years, according to their assessment that he had been on earth. The whole thing was complimenting, yet somehow annoying.

Lana also noticed the boys and men who looked extra long at her. It was as if her near Adonislooking companion had suddenly turned her into a Goddess. She knew she felt different, full of energy and alive.

Had becoming part arachnid done this to her, she wondered. *And, would this feeling continue, or would it go away after she had adjusted to the changes her body was going through?*

She rubbed her hand across the miniature hourglass mark that adorned a small area next to her navel. Then, she quietly and inconspicuously pulled her shirt to the side and looked at it. Briefly, she touched it with her fingertips; then, quickly covered it. Looking up, she noticed they were in the section of the carnival that exhibited a number of games.

Oh shoot, she suddenly thought. *It's Evan's birthday.*

Lana quickly glanced around, looking for something she might be able to win at. Basketball—no. Tossing rings onto a bottle—no. Then, she noticed a game that required concentration and a steady hand. The large billboard sign above the stand flashed the name of the game in red—The Electric Eel.

"Let's try that game," she pointed to the stand.

The older gentlemen, behind the long wooden box, displaying numerous pieces of twisted metal, smiled and held up a beautifully dressed Victorian doll—an enticement to draw her interest and convince her, or Evan, to play.

The doll was exquisite and Lana sighed. She wasn't playing for herself, but for a gift for Evan. She glanced at the array of items displayed on the wall behind the man.

There was a lovely floral print, a huge pink bear in a skirt and hat, a skateboard, two small brass lamps, and a variety of other items, Evan probably wouldn't want or need.

She suddenly caught glimpse of a cowboy hat sitting in the corner on one of the shelves to the far right. It was black leather with a plain black band around the crown. It was perfect!

"So, little missy, whaddya see that you'd like?" The man held the doll before her. "Isn't she beautiful?" He smoothed the delicate lace on the doll's dress.

"Yes, she is beautiful," Lana answered. "But…" she glanced over at Evan who just smiled warmly at her and handed the man a five dollar bill—enough for two games. "I might pick something else if I win."

The man's eyes cut in the direction of the pink bear. "Ah, a nice choice," he stated as he nodded his head. "Here…" He picked up the metal wand and handed it to her. It had a loop at the end and was attached by a string to the spiral figure of metal that she had to wind it around without touching. If she touched the spiral figure it would irritably glow red—a sign she had made contact with the wand and that she had lost the game.

"No cheating," Evan suddenly whispered softly into the back of her hair. "If you don't win what you want, I'll get it for you."

Lana turned and stared into his perfect eyes. "I will win. You'll see." She whipped back around and focused on the spiral figure before her." Then, she paused, realizing she needed an excuse to get Evan away from the game, so she could get his hat without him knowing.

"Now, I need to focus on the game." She stepped away from him. "I can't be distracted."

Evan followed her footsteps and his lips slipped within her hair and touched her ear. "Why *me*, distract *you*?"

"Stop!" She playfully giggled. "Now, go get us a drink or something, so I can concentrate."

Evan placed his arms around her waist and teasingly stated, "I'm not so sure I wanna leave you alone here. Do you think it's safe?"

"Of course it is." She playfully elbowed him. "Now go, while I win you that big pink bear.

Evan's gaze narrowed. "It couldn't be brown?"

"No," she firmly stated. "I think you'd like the pink one."

Evan grimaced. "I think I'll go get that drink."

Lana softly laughed and turned her attention back to the game. Picking up the wand, she briefly held it in her hand. It was cold and hard and anxiety at winning the hat for Evan made her even sweatier than the 90 degree temperatures that continued to hang into the late afternoon.

I can do this, she thought. *I can do it*!

Holding her breath, she held the wand over the spiral figure then slowly and carefully she moved it along the twists and bends of the metal. "Come on," she whispered to herself. "Come on!" Her hand slightly trembled and she breathed in.

Suddenly, the spiral figure began to zap and spark, glow bright red—an indication she had touched the metal.

"Shoot!" Her heart sank as she stomped her foot and glanced up at the man. He was nonchalantly leaning against a pole and smiling at her.

"Welp, young lady, you have one more try. Your boyfriend paid for two games for ya. So, go ahead and give it another shot." He hit a button beneath the stand with his foot and a mild thrumming sounded from beneath her.

Lana briefly stared at him, mild surprise upon her countenance, either from the fact that she didn't know she had another game coming to her, or, just a reaction to his referring to Evan as her boyfriend. Either way, it didn't matter.

All she knew was she needed to win the hat.

A young boy, possibly twelve or thirteen, scurried up beside her to the next spiral figure. He was followed by an older sister.

"Hurry up, Liz. I wanna play this game before we have to meet Mom and Dad."

"Okay, okay," Liz remarked. "Just hold your horses." Quickly, she dug into her pants pocket and pulled out two dollars and fifty cents. Then, she handed the money to the man who eagerly took it and slipped it into a pouch strapped around his waist.

Lana watched the young boy as he held the wand over the figure. Then, impatiently running it along the metal, he quickly lost the game.

"Aw!" He laid the wand down and hurriedly turned to his sister. "I can't win *anything*."

"That's okay," Liz stated as she ruffled his hair. "I'll win you something later. Now, come on; Mom and Dad are waiting."

Lana quietly watched as the two ran off and disappeared out of sight. She immediately began to feel lonely, which was also followed by a feeling of guilt—guilt for being at a carnival having fun, while, God only knew, what was happening to her younger brother. Also, her parents had just been killed. As soon as she got the hat, she would ask Evan if they could leave.

Picking up the wand and concentrating extra hard, she slowly ran it along the spiral figure using every human ability she possessed. Perspiration beaded her forehead and her hand began to shake.

"Come on," she whispered beneath her breath. "I can do this!"

Little by little Lana's gaze narrowed, and her slightly trembling hand became more nimble and moved with assuredness. The gap between the wand's inner loop and the spiral figure appeared to have widened; and, the cool of the wand's handle was no longer cold to the touch or a foreign object within her grasp. Instead, it was now an extension of her hand, a fine-tuned instrument she could have used to perform the most intricate of surgery.

It was the arachnid beast coming alive within her with the urgency to win the game. Within half a second, the wand reached the bottom of the spiral figure and a blue light flashed brilliantly before her eyes. She had won.

The game attendant, who had been assisting another customer, turned in surprise and looked at Lana and the wand lying in the winning position.

"Well, lookie here," he called out for those passing by to hear. "We have ourselves a winner, folks!" Quickly, he turned and grabbed the pink bear off the shelf and held it up for everyone to see. "Big prizes! Bears, skateboards, and much, much more!" He handed the bear to Lana.

"Here you go, sweetheart."

Lana shook her head. "No, sir. I would like the cowboy hat. Could I have that instead?"

"Why sure, little lady." Stretching, he reached up and grabbed the hat.

"Could I have that in a bag please?" Lana asked.

"Sure," he answered as he reached beneath the counter, pulled out a brown paper bag and placed the hat inside. "I hope he likes it," he stated with a wink.

Lana smiled. "I'm sure he will."

Suddenly, a voice lowly spoke behind her; the words were warm in the back of her hair. "Oh, I know he will."

"Evan?" Lana turned around afraid he had seen his gift. However, it wasn't Evan who was standing pressed tightly against her. It was Marty Brow.

Lana spun. And, nearly tripping over her feet, she moved quickly in the direction Evan had gone. Marty stayed just a few feet behind her, keeping pace with her anxious steps.

Her heart banged within her chest and the tiny beads of perspiration upon her forehead immediately became droplets of sweat.

She moved through a crowd of high school kids who had just arrived by bus. *Where did* they *come from?* It would be hard to spot Evan; he would blend right in.

Using her arachnid senses, Lana concentrated on the different scents, especially the smell of blood. She would be able to find Evan by his blood. However, her sense of smell continued to be diverted by the scent of another black widow—one that was within close proximity. It wasn't Spence's—his was strong, pungent, a scent she would never forget or wanted to smell again.

The odor moved away from her as she pushed her way through the crowd. It became fainter, a mere whiff of something or someone her arachnid would like to hunt. But, as for her human self, the only scent she wanted to smell right now was Evan's.

She could also sense that there were others who had

joined Marty. They had positioned themselves in a V behind her and seemed to be driving her toward the outer limits of the carnival. *Evan, where are you?*

Breaking free of the crowd, she continued in no particular direction, running blindly toward the trailer park ahead.

Chapter 21

Evan had smelled the scent of another arachnid's blood as soon as he had left Lana and her overwhelming scent. He knew the other arachnid was associated with Spence; he could smell Spence's scent all over them.

"Where are you, you little bastard?" He moved quickly through the crowd of teens and their chaperones, searching diligently for the other black widow, wanting to reach them before they reached Lana. The cup of pink lemonade he had just bought her sloshed about and doused his hand.

"Crap!" He quickly tossed the drink into a receptacle and pressed onward.

The scent was quickly becoming weak, moving rapidly away from him and the carnival. They must be in a vehicle and driving away.

Immediately, Evan circled back around and headed in the direction of where he had left Lana at the game. She should be finished by now; then, maybe they could leave soon. He had a bad feeling about this and wanted to get her home.

He arrived at the game which was surrounded now by various players. The carnival had suddenly become crowded and Lana was nowhere to be seen.

Pressing through the people, Evan attempted to get

the man's attention. However, he was busy assisting two young teenage girls, who stopped and smiled at him. Ignoring their overzealous grins, Evan yelled to the man.

"Sir!"

The squealing and talking of people, and ruckus of the other games, drown out Evan's attempt at getting the man's attention. He tried again.

"Excuse me, Sir!"

The man turned and looked at him.

"What happened to the young girl who was here just a minute ago playing?"

The man shrugged his shoulders. "I don't know," he shouted back. "She just left with some young fella."

"What?" Evan turned the color of milk.

The man handed the two young girls their change, then hit a switch under the counter.

"Yeah, she won somethin', then hurried away with some guy in tow."

"Shit!" Evan spun around and pushed his way through the people.

"Damn it! I knew I should've stayed with her!" Indifferent to the number of stares, he rapidly scaled a large elephant statue, stood on its back and looked around. Taking a deep breath, he caught Lana's scent on the opposite end of the carnival; she was heading in the direction of the trailer park that sat on the outskirts of town. He could also see, from where he was, four men pursuing her.

"You rotten bastards!" They had used someone or something as a ploy to draw him away, while these ya-hoos went after Lana. More than likely they were associated with Spence.

There were too many people around for him to transform; and yet he still would be unable to call upon the beast with Lana being driven in the direction of the trailer park.

Evan's feet hit the ground with a thud, as those watching oohed and aahed then applauded thinking he was part of a circus act employed by the carnival. Irritably, he glanced around at the crowd then took off running in the direction of where Lana was being led.

Lana quickly ducked behind the last trailer which was hooked by electrical cords and hydraulic hoses to two abandoned food concession stands that were sitting by themselves.

The sound of her heart banged within her ears; and, the footsteps of the four men following her clashed like thunder upon the ground. She could feel her eight arachnid legs punching through the skin on her back.

"Oh God," she whispered beneath her breath, while she wanted to cry out or scream, do anything to alleviate the pain that was abrupt and unexpected. Instead, she bit at her lower lip until she tasted blood. And, stumbling out from behind the trailer, she made her way toward the nearby trailer park. The sign at the entrance read: “Lynn’s Trailer Court.”

Lana kicked her feet outward trying to break the strands of webbing that were quickly consuming her. “No, not now!” She pulled at the threads with her free hand while the hand that held the bag containing Evan’s hat quickly became caught within the webbing and rapidly disappeared inside her growing cocoon.

Stumbling forward, she tripped into a nearby fence and the momentum sent her tumbling to the ground. The air left her body and she groaned.

For a moment, she lay dazed, listening to the echo of her own labored breaths and the sound of the men’s raspy breathing. They were rapidly closing in behind her; she needed to get on the other side of the fence. Grabbing a post with her free hand, she tried to scoot herself up to standing position. “Come on!” She kicked with her feet trying to break free.

Suddenly, she heard Evan’s voice.

“Run, Lana! Run!”

“I can’t!” she cried. Losing her grip on the fence, she fell to the ground. Evan suddenly scooped her up into his arms.

“Shit! I knew this would happen.” He cursed at himself, hating that he had left her alone and in danger.

“I’m sorry,” she exclaimed through a tear-filled gaze.

He looked into her eyes and pulled her tighter

to him. “Save it till we get outta here; then, I’ll be apologizing to you.” He headed for the clearing and a patch of heavy brush. “We need to hide. I don’t know how much longer I can run in this heat. Plus, those guys are carrying guns.”

“Guns?” Lana stared up at him.

“Yeah,” he replied as he hurriedly scanned the area. “They must’ve been hiding them in their coats. I don’t know who they are; but, I’m almost certain they’re associated with Spence.”

Evan raced in the direction of the high weeds and brush and slammed to a halt as he reached the edge of the precipice overlooking the river. He groaned. Then, hurriedly evaluating the situation, the long drop to the water and the jagged rocks below, he spun around to head in the opposite direction.

One of the men, resembling a scarecrow, suddenly burst through the brush. “They’re over here!” He wheezed and bent to take a breath.

One of the others responded, “I know, I got em!”

Evan spun back again to face the river. “Hold on, Lana.”

Suddenly a shot rang out and his body pitched forward.

“No!” Lana screamed as she desperately clung to him and they raced at lightning speed toward the rocks below. Terrified, she closed her eyes and attempted to concentrate, do something to draw the beast within her to the surface—save them from being crushed against the jagged boulders below.

"Concentrate! Concentrate!" The words screamed from her throat as sweat poured from her body.

Suddenly, her arachnid beast burst from within her human skin; however, she was too late and they crashed to the ground below.

Look for the next volume of the Spidey Legs Lana trilogy!

SUMMER 2010

Also, check out these other great works by Tessa LaRock:

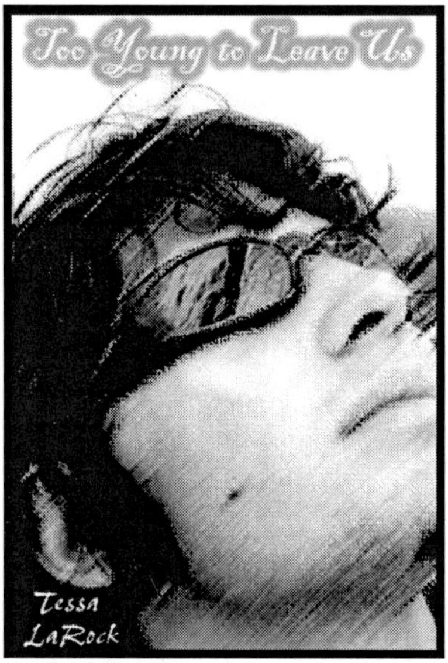

LaVergne, TN USA
08 November 2010
203963LV00002B/44/P

9 780982 107584